"Mind if I cut in?"

The next thing Edney knew she was gliding around the dance floor in her employer's arms.

"You've been leading Felix on all evening!" Saville snarled.

"You've only been here a little over an hour, so how in blazes would you know?" she challenged furiously.

"It doesn't take a minute to read an enticing glance here, an encouraging smile there," he clipped aggressively.

"Well, you'd certainly know about that," she said sarcastically, not doubting that he, with his wealth of experience of women, was a past master at reading all signals! She informed him snappily, "I've had enough dancing."

"It isn't over yet. I'll tell you when!" Saville had the nerve to inform her curtly.

"You may be my boss Monday to Friday," Edney hissed. "But we're not in the office now!"

From boardroom...to bride and groom!

Dear Reader,

Welcome to the first book in our MARRYING THE BOSS miniseries.

Over the following months, some of your favorite Harlequin Romance® authors will be bringing you a variety of tantalizing stories about love in the workplace!

Falling for the boss can mean trouble, so our gorgeous heroes and lively heroines all struggle to resist their feelings of attraction for each other. But somehow love always ends up top of the agenda. And it isn't just a nine-to-five affair.... Mixing business with pleasure carries on after hours—and ends in marriage!

Happy Reading!

The Editors

Look out for the second title in our
MARRYING THE BOSS series:
Boardroom Proposal by Margaret Way
Harlequin Romance® #3540

Agenda:
Attraction!
Jessica Steele

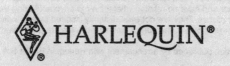

TORONTO • NEW YORK • LONDON
AMSTERDAM • PARIS • SYDNEY • HAMBURG
STOCKHOLM • ATHENS • TOKYO • MILAN • MADRID
PRAGUE • WARSAW • BUDAPEST • AUCKLAND

ISBN 0-373-03536-5

AGENDA: ATTRACTION!

First North American Publication 1999.

CHAPTER ONE

EDNEY was not enjoying the party. She was there with Tony Watson, a first date—and a last. She had known Tony for some months. Being selective—some said choosy—she had turned down many of his invitations to go out. But he had always remained pleasant, and when her friend Deborah had said that she and her husband Jeremy were having a party, insisting that Edney must attend, Deborah had also added, 'Men seem to be in short supply. Can you bring one of your own from that panting pack that follow you around?'

'You exaggerate!' Edney had laughed. But Tony Watson had seemed quite safe, and she had invited him. That was then. Now… She had spent most of the evening trying to keep him at arm's length and in avoiding the innuendo that seemed to be in every word he spoke. She wanted to go home. The trouble with that was that Deborah and Jeremy had worked so hard on the party and it was still early. The last thing she wanted was to offend her hosts. Equally the last thing she wanted was to drive home with Tony Watson. Though since it was in Tony's car they had arrived, there did not seem to be much alternative to the fact that with Tony she would have to depart.

Realising she could not stay in Deborah's bathroom for ever, Edney reluctantly rejoined the party. Nothing much had changed, she observed, people dancing, people eating, drinking, laughing. By any standards it was a good party.

She saw Tony making his relentless way over to where she stood, and, in an endeavour to hide her ex-

5

pression, looked away—straight into the eyes of a tall, dark-haired man who must have just come in; she would swear he had not been at the party earlier.

He seemed to stand out from all of the rest; he had dark eyes, was sophisticated and somewhere in his midthirties, and if he'd been there before she knew she would have noticed him. He was just the sort of man that people *did* notice. Something about him, an air... His gaze, unsmiling, was steady on her.

'Crowded in there, was it?' Tony's voice drew her attention abruptly back to him.

'Er—sorry?' she queried, not with him, her mind still filled with the latecomer to the party.

'You were a long time powdering your nose,' Tony hinted.

She tried to smile. 'Girl talk,' she excused, thinking the subject dead.

'Comparing notes?' he leered, 'How many stars did I get?'

Grow up, Tony! Grief, he was twenty-eight. Of the two of them she, at twenty-two, felt the more mature. She'd like to bet the latecomer could never act in such an asinine way.

She was unsure why she thought that, but, unable to help it, she flicked a glance his way—he was no longer alone. True, there *was* a surfeit of females at the party, but did half a dozen of them have to crowd around *him*?

Oh, hang it, she was letting her irritation with Tony run over. Edney took herself in hand. 'Dance?' she enquired of her escort. She had, after all, she reminded herself, invited him along, and the music being played was such that he had no need to touch her.

Somehow, touch her he did. Edney pushed him away, in no mind to be polite about his octopus mood. She was getting cross; she could feel it. But she smiled, or at least her mouth did.

Tony pulled her close. Stiflingly close. She'd had enough! She shoved him abruptly from her, experienced a brief moment when good manners got through to remind her not to upset Deborah's party, and, finding herself near the open French windows, escaped that way.

Unfortunately, Tony Watson followed her. 'What did I do?' he questioned in hurt tones.

'I don't enjoy being pawed around!' she told him stiffly, moving from him into the large garden.

'Hells bells, I hardly touched you!' he protested, following her. She had no intention of arguing. He'd been touching her all evening. 'You're still playing hard to get,' Tony went on, his tone changing. 'For all you must fancy me, or you wouldn't have asked me to come with you, you're still wanting me to beg.'

Oh, grief! She wanted to go home. She had thought him a friend. She guessed she was more naive than she'd thought. She halted and turned. 'Look, Tony,' she began firmly—but didn't get to say anything more for many long, frightening seconds, because, misreading the signs completely, Tony made a grab for her.

His kiss landed somewhere between her cheek and the corner of her mouth. She pushed and struggled, more angry than frightened. His grip on her tightened—she could barely breathe.

'Let go of me!' she yelled, struggling so his mouth should not make contact with hers.

'You're loving this, aren't you?' He refused to take no for an answer as she struggled to be free, seeming instead to be growing more excited, and taking encouragement from her attempts to extricate herself from his lascivious grip.

Suddenly Edney became aware of how far they had moved away from the house. Disturbingly, she also noticed that they were screened by some high bushes—and that there was no one else around! It was then that she went from angry to worried. This far away, and with the music playing inside, the chances of anyone hearing her if she screamed were remote. Oh, help, no one could see them, no one would hear if...

But someone was around, someone had seen them, she discovered. Someone had come out for a stroll in the garden, and had seen, had heard—that much was obvious when, as she still fought to be free, a cool, detached kind of voice casually drawled, 'From where I'm standing, I'd say the lady is more hating than loving it.'

Startled to hear that cultured voice, and realising they were being observed, Tony Watson loosened his grip on her. Edney did not waste a second. In no time she was out of his arms and had put herself nearer to the man she at once recognised as the latecomer to the party.

Ignoring Tony, her agitation rapidly dropping, it was to the stranger that she addressed her remarks. 'I'm going home!' she stated shortly—and realised she must be more upset than she'd thought she was. As if he'd be interested where she was going, for goodness' sake! 'Oh, botheration!' she muttered, more to herself this time than to him. 'I came in his car!'

'Not to worry, I'll give you a lift,' the man offered easily.

'But—you can't leave!' she protested, and at once knew that this man was totally unused to being told what he could and could not do.

'I can't?' he queried. 'You know something I don't?'

'You've only just got here!' she found herself explaining, getting herself more together by the second.

'You noticed?' He seemed amused.

She liked him. 'I'm exceptionally observant,' she responded.

Tony, at that point, regained his second wind. 'She came with me!' He decided to make his presence felt. 'I'm taking her home.'

The stranger didn't even bother to look at him. 'No, you're not,' he said with quiet finality—no argument. And, with his eyes holding Edney's in the light of that summer night, he said, 'Shall we go?'

Edney went with him back inside the house, where her new escort was at once buttonholed by a couple she had been introduced to earlier, and who, it seemed, particularly wanted to have a word with him.

By that time Edney's innate good manners had surfaced, and she excused herself and went to find her hosts. 'I've had a lovely time,' she smiled.

'You're not going! It's early!' Deborah protested.

There was nothing for it. 'I made an error of judgement with Tony,' she explained, still managing to smile so her hostess would know it was nothing terribly serious. 'Would you mind very much if I left him behind?'

'He's nothing Jeremy can't handle,' Deborah assured her. 'I'll get you a taxi.'

'No need,' Edney said quickly. 'That man, the one talking to—er—Kate and Cyril—he's offered me a lift.' Deborah looked over to the trio and Edney went on, 'Um—he is—okay, is he?'

'This time your judgement's spot-on,' Deborah replied. 'Jeremy's known him for years—they were at university together. He promised he'd try and look in to say hello, but we knew he wouldn't stay for very long. You'll be quite safe with him,' Deborah was at pains to reassure her. 'He's got half the women in this room drooling over him—he's not the smallest need to grab where he can.' Edney rather thought she had evidence of that for herself when while watching as he made his way over, she observed how he was waylaid several times. 'Besides which, that wouldn't be his style.'

Eventually they made it out to his sleek and expensive car. Edney gave him directions to where she lived, a half-hour away but still on the outskirts of London, and they were on their way. Where Tony Watson was she neither knew nor cared.

Several minutes elapsed with nothing very much in the way of conversation passing between them. That was when Edney began to think that, since this man was putting himself out to give her a lift—having already put himself out when, just by being there, he had rescued her from Tony's unwanted over-amorous attentions—it wouldn't hurt her to make a little polite conversation. The thing was, though, and she would swear that it had never happened to her before, she felt oddly tongue-tied—shy—now that they were alone.

Ridiculous! she told herself stoutly, and, since both Deborah and Jeremy had assumed they had introduced themselves to each other, she opened her mouth, fully intending to ask him his name. But, to her dismay, she heard herself enquire, 'Your wife wasn't able to come with you this evening, Mr—?' She broke off, shaken more by her question than the fact that she didn't have a name to tack on to the 'Mr'.

'Didn't Deborah tell you?' he enquired, a man who apparently asked the questions, and didn't go in much for answering any.

'What?' she questioned back—uncertain which of her questions he wasn't answering: the 'are you married' one, or the 'what comes after Mr' one.

'When you were checking me out,' he replied, which in her view was no reply at all. Was he offended that she had checked him out? Oh, crumbs—generally, she wasn't having a very good evening. But she soon realised that she had not offended him for he demanded, his tone toughening, 'You did check me out? You haven't, like some lamb to the slaughter, just got in this car with me, without first checking...?'

'According to Deborah,' Edney rushed in before his tone could get any tougher—for no reason she could think of, she didn't want him to be short and sharp with her, 'I'll be quite safe with you.' She forbore to add the rest—that he'd got half the women in the room drooling over him and that he had not the slightest need to grab where he could.

He seemed to relax a little after that. 'Do you work in the City?' he asked, changing the subject completely.

Edney was glad to finish with the old one, and very nearly blurted out her joy, the excitement she felt about the new job she was starting on Monday, and how fortunate she considered she was in beating the other applicants for it. Just in time, though, she managed to stop herself from declaring proudly that she was going to work for I. L. Engineering and Design. He was a sophisticated man, for heaven's sake. And if looks—clothes, demeanour—not to mention that his old university friend, Jeremy, was quite something in the business world—were anything to go by, then she wouldn't be at all surprised if he was quite something in the City himself.

'I'm—er—between jobs at the moment,' she replied, hoping he would think that her delay in answering stemmed from embarrassment that she didn't have a job, rather than that she was on the brink of gauchely blurting out how elated she was to have landed the job as an assistant to a PA. 'Oh, we turn right here,' she directed him quickly.

As they went up the drive to the large old house set in its own grounds, she realised that, when the fact was indeed very different, he could be forgiven for thinking, as the car lights lit up the building, that as her family lived in such a large property, maybe she had no need to go out to work.

The house was in total darkness—her father saving on electricity again! 'Your parents have gone to bed,' her escort commented easily as he got out of the car with her and walked with her to the solid front door.

'My father,' she answered. 'My parents are divorced.'

'Where does the man you were with tonight fit in?' he wanted to know.

'He doesn't. Not any more. Not that he did particularly anyway.' She wished she hadn't got started on this but somehow felt compelled to carry on. 'There's a group of us. Just friends. Tony sort of fell in with our group some months ago. I thought he was safe—and asked him to come with me to Deborah and Jeremy's party.' Whew! She doubly wished she hadn't got started on this—she was gabbling, sounding as though she'd had her mouth taped up for a month! 'Are you coming in for coffee?' she asked abruptly.

'Not when you ask so prettily.'

'I'm sorry,' she apologised at once; she hadn't meant to invite him in for coffee, and certainly not so snappily—but had needed to change the subject. 'I think I'm still a little wound up.'

'Don't worry about it,' he soothed, 'Not all men are like your ex-friend, Tony.'

'I know,' she answered quietly—and discovered that this man was very unlike her ex-friend when, his head coming nearer, and as if to rid her of the memory of Tony's lascivious, vile lips, he gently laid his mouth on hers in a whisper of a tender, healing kiss.

He didn't otherwise touch her and, as Edney stood riveted, just staring, he stepped back. 'I'm catching an early flight tomorrow,' he informed her. While her brain awoke to suggest he had just turned down her offer of coffee, he asked, 'Do you feel inclined to let me have your phone number?'

Did she feel inclined? Yes! After that touch of his mouth on hers, in that kiss which had demanded nothing, but which had spoken of the inner sensitivity of the man? Yes, oh, yes!

She almost said yes straight away. But in view of his question about where did Tony fit in, she felt able to rephrase a question he hadn't answered earlier. 'Are you married?' she asked forthrightly.

'A woman with scruples!' he mocked softly.

'You've been mixing with the wrong sort!' she laughed, but refused to give him her phone number until he'd answered her question.

'Not married,' he owned. 'Though I've nothing against marriage—for others.'

'You've never been in love?' she found herself asking. 'Sorry—you must be wanting to dash. You've got a plane to catch.' Grief—where was her brain?—starting an in-depth discussion on his love life on her doorstep? Not, she guessed, that he'd take part unless he felt like it. 'Goodnight!' she said quickly.

'Phone number?'

Was she suddenly addle-headed, or what? Swiftly she gave it to him. He did not write it down. He won't remember; I'm sure he won't, some inner part of her regretted. 'Thanks very much for bringing me home.'

'Goodnight,' he said—and was gone.

Edney lay awake for a long time in her bed that night. He wouldn't remember; he wouldn't. That grieved her a little. For someone who rarely, if ever, did impulsive things—such as going out on a date with some man she barely knew—it oddly perturbed her that the man who'd come to her aid at the party might not make contact with her again.

When Edney awakened on Sunday morning, she was glad to find that her brain had awakened with her. And, although thoughts of the man who had kindly given her a lift home were instantly in her head, she at once scorned that she was in any way upset because she might not see him again.

And, for heaven's sake, if he wanted to see her again he knew where she lived! If his memory was so shaky that he couldn't remember, then he could always ask Deborah. Anyhow, since she assumed he had flown off on holiday this morning, she was unlikely to see him again for quite some while. He could be away for a month or more for all she knew. She might have wished him a happy holiday, though.

She went downstairs to start breakfast. Her father, an inborn grumbler, was already up. 'There's not enough bacon for two,' he grumbled.

She loved him dearly. 'I'll have an egg.'

'I think I'm coming down with a cold.'

'Are you going to church this morning?'

'Have you been there lately? It's like an ice-box in there.'

'It's summer!'

'Tell that to the weatherman! Are you going to your mother's next weekend?'

More to keep the peace than anything, Edney paid an overnight visit to her mother in Bristol every other Saturday. 'You know I am,' she replied, and when, having a face for every occasion, her father looked exceedingly downcast, she added, 'I won't if you'd rather I didn't.'

At once he bridled. 'What—and have her ringing up here asking where you are?' Her parents' mutual acrimony was still going on eleven years after their divorce.

'One egg or two?'

'There's no need to be extravagant.'

Edney laughed. She'd lived with him long enough to see through his crusty exterior. He gave her a sideways look and she knew he was smiling inside, for all he would never let on. 'Didn't think much of that Tony who called for you last night!' he stated, determined, it seemed, to be a grouch.

'I didn't think much of him myself. Er—someone else brought me home.'

'That's what your mother taught you, was it? Go to a party with one beau and come home with another.'

Beau! Agreed, her father was sixty-four, and sometimes old-fashioned. But *beau!* 'He—er—rescued me from a fate worse than death,' she dropped out lightly.

'*What?*' Charles Rayner roared, and, had Edney needed evidence that she was a much-loved daughter—her father would die before he'd dream of telling her—she had it in his furious expression. 'Where does he live, this man, this Tony? I'll go and see him! Damned if I won't! It *was* he who—?'

'Oh, Dad, I'm sorry. I didn't mean to upset you!' Grief, she hadn't. She had just meant to laugh him out of his determined sour mood; it worked sometimes. And, although Tony Watson's attempts to kiss her against her wishes and the ensuing tussle hadn't been at all funny, she had been able to put it behind her. 'It wasn't anywhere near as bad as I made it sound. And anyhow, this man, the one who brought me home, he was there to sort Tony out.'

'Hit him, did he?'

'He didn't have to.'

'I would have done.'

'You're terrific!' Edney smiled.

'What's his name? I'll write to him.'

'Who?' she asked startled.

'The man who brought you home. Your knight in shining armour.'

Edney laughed; her father had calmed down again. 'He wasn't riding a white horse,' she chuckled. 'And I don't know his name.'

'Your mother's idea of educating a young lady into

the manners of the day has been sadly at fault,' he declared. And, as crusty as ever, he added, 'You should always get a chap's name, Edney—if only so that you can sue him later.' He grinned suddenly, as if amused—and Sunday got under way.

It was a busy day for Edney. As well as preparing a roast, she spent some time in her room, reviewing her wardrobe.

I. L. Engineering and Design, her new employers as of tomorrow, was an exceedingly smart outfit. Her new job was as assistant to the PA to the head of that outfit and, because the job had been advertised within the group as well as outside, Edney was fully aware of her good fortune in being appointed to be assistant to Annette Lewis. The previous assistant had been promoted to PA to one of the I. L. directors.

Edney had been working as a secretary in civil engineering, and had been amazed when she'd seen the salary advertised. Though once she had sent off her letter of application, and had been invited initially for an interview with head of personnel, she'd learned more about the work involved, and the high salary offered had taken second place. She wanted this job. The work sounded stimulating, interesting, a challenge. By the end of that interview she had been truly keen to have the job—for its own sake. It would mean hard work, but she'd felt certain, if allowed, she could do it.

As the next few days had gone by, Edney had begun to see that it was all a pipe dream. Her schooling had been fractured by the battle that had gone on as her parents fought for custody of her. First she had lived with her mother in Bristol, and then with her father, and then with her mother again. Then, when she was fifteen, her mother had married a widower with a son a few years older than Edney.

'That's it!' her father had declared. 'You're coming

back to live with me. I'm not having some other man bringing up my daughter. Your mother bled me dry with that divorce settlement—outrageously unfair,' he'd complained, 'and she's not having you as well. Damn the expense. I'll get the best lawyers and take her to court again.'

Pulled both ways, and loving both her parents, Edney had been by then very conscious of her mother's determination to fight her former husband to the death over every issue, large or small. This time, however, maybe because of her new-found love, soon her new-found husband, her mother's priorities seemed to have temporarily shifted. And, although the matter had gone to court, this time she'd given in far more easily. Edney, on condition she saw her mother every two weeks, had gone to live with her father.

And her father, having folded his architect's business after the divorce settlement cleaned him out, had vowed then that he would work sufficiently only for his and his daughter's needs. He had no intention of slogging his guts out only for Edney's mother to find some new way of getting her hands on his earnings. He still hadn't trusted his ex-wife even when she had remarried, so worked no harder. Though, when Edney had told him she wanted to do some business training, he'd somehow managed to find the funds from somewhere to send her to the best of business colleges.

Edney, on her part, had worked hard and had done well, her results showing that she would have no trouble in getting a job at the end of her training. Would they be good enough to get her the job of assistant to Annette Lewis?

Edney had barely been able to bring herself to open the envelope when the letter she had been watching for arrived. But, expecting a polite 'Thank you for coming

for interview but…' kind of letter, she'd learned she had
been short-listed for the job.

Annette Lewis, a thorough professional of around
forty, had sat in at the second interview with the head
of personnel and Edney had taken to the PA straight
away. She'd felt that the interview went well. But she'd
had all of an agonising week to wait before she'd been
called for a third interview.

This time her interview had been in Annette Lewis's
office. The office that Edney would share—if she was
successful. And she'd discovered right there and then
that she was successful, that she had been chosen!

'You mean the job's mine!' she'd gasped.

'If you'd like it?' Annette had smiled, going on, 'The
decision, subject to Mr Craythorne's approval, to offer
you the post was made some days ago. But today was
the first space in Mr Craythorne's diary for him to see
you personally.'

'He wants to interview me himself?' Edney had questioned. My word, Saville Craythorne, the man Annette
was PA to, was boss of the whole shoot! Oh, she did so
hope he liked her!

'He intended to interview you,' Annette had agreed,
'though, unfortunately, Mr Butler, his deputy, has been
taken acutely ill, and Saville—Mr Craythorne—' she'd
corrected, 'has gone with him to the hospital—instructing me to offer you a temporary post, to be made permanent after three months if you're as good as I've said
you are.'

Edney had gone home beaming. She was extremely
sorry that this Mr Butler was ill, but had realised that
Saville Craythorne must have implicit trust in Annette
Lewis's ability to select just the right person for his office—not that he'd had much choice, she'd supposed,
with a flap going on.

She'd smiled at the word 'flap'; Annette had seemed

totally unflappable, and, while instructing Edney that she would earn every penny of her pay—no leaving work on the stroke of five if there was something needing to be completed—had informed her she would have to be available, reliable, tactful—the smooth running of Saville Craythorne's office was essential.

Annette had gone on to explain that she planned to take a holiday in a couple of months' time so, given that Edney would have to give her present employer a month's notice, she would have to learn quickly when she got there, because she would be in charge of the running of the office during Annette's absence.

The PA had smiled then. 'But you've no need to worry; my previous assistant still works in the building. Pippa will be here to help if you need her. Though I'm sure you won't.' She smiled again. 'One of the reasons I chose you was because you seem to me to be calm and unlikely to get in a dither.'

Edney thought about that interview when, on Sunday afternoon, she doubly checked the outfit she would wear for her first day at I. L. Engineering and Design. She thought, too, of the man who had brought her home from the party last night. She thought about him a lot. Would he get in touch with her again? Think about something else, do. He was probably sunning himself on some sundrenched beach at this very moment, a glass of something cool in one hand—a cool blonde in the other.

Edney stretched an involuntary hand up to her own long tresses. They were red. How did he feel about redheaded, blue-eyed females with pale complexions? Gracious, as if she cared! The possibility that he would remember her after his month-long holiday—or for however long he planned to be away—was extremely remote. So stop thinking about him, do! Go and polish your shoes.

Her first day at I. L. Engineering was truly a revelation

into how big business worked. Though had she been a little nervous about meeting the chairman of the company, the man who had the large, plush next-door office, Edney found her nervousness was wasted. He wasn't in for business that day, or even expected.

'Saville's in Milan at the moment.' Annette informed her. 'You'll meet him next week. Meantime we'll take advantage of his absence to get you familiar with what goes on.'

Edney reeled out of I. L. Engineering that night with her head spinning. She walked to the car park with Annette, observed without envy that Annette drove this year's model of a saloon, and drove out of there in her reliable Mini wondering when, if ever, she might be able to afford a new car.

Tuesday seemed busier than Monday—there was a lot to learn. While Edney started to have the feeling that she would never be able to cope when Annette went on holiday, she managed to maintain her calm-and-unlikely-to-dither front, which was one of the reasons she had got the job. Again, she went home with her head spinning.

On Wednesday, a little daylight started to filter into the mass of correspondence, facts, figures, and the pleasant tactfulness required to deal with senior members of the company. Mr Craythorne rang and spoke directly and at some length with Annette. Edney went home that night realising that she had enjoyed her day, and that she was starting to enjoy her work. Yesterday she had been beginning to doubt that she had done the right thing in leaving her previous unchallenging, not to say dull, job. Tonight, she was glad she had made the move—she was starting to be very very taken with this fresh challenge.

The phone rang just as she finished her meal. 'Your mother!' her father suspected sourly. And, wickedly, as Edney got up to answer it, he said, 'Give her my love.'

Edney gave him a look that spoke volumes and went

out to the hall phone. 'Hello?' she greeted her mother brightly. Only the caller wasn't her mother.

'You sound cheerful! You must have recovered from Saturday night,' answered a voice she felt she would know anywhere.

'You're back!' she exclaimed—that was a brief holiday!

'Not yet. I'll be home Friday. I know it's short notice—I wondered if you'd be free to have dinner with me on Friday?'

Why was her heart racing like this? She'd been out to dinner on many a Friday evening. She felt too excited anyway to be evasive. 'I'll look forward to it,' she smiled.

She rather thought he was smiling too as he replied, 'I'll call for you at seven-thirty.'

Oddly she felt a need to get herself together. 'Till then,' she said, and whether he was inclined to chat on or not, she put down her phone handset.

Naturally she had to tell her father about her call. 'Find out his name yet?'

Astonished, she stared at her parent. 'I forgot!' And, in receipt of her father's 'women are dim' look, added smartly, 'But he doesn't know mine either.'

Well, not unless he'd taken the trouble to ring Deborah or Jeremy to find out—and she somehow couldn't see him doing that. Edney gave some thought to ringing Deborah herself to ask his name but decided against it. Deborah was six years older than herself, and the two had become good friends when Deborah had made several visits to consult Edney's father over some architectural work he was doing for herself and Jeremy. Edney had already written a note of thanks for the party, so couldn't use that as an excuse for ringing.

Besides which as Edney went to make a swift examination of her wardrobe to find something suitable in which to dine with the dark-eyed, dark-haired man she so clearly remembered, she confessed to still feeling a little shaky after his unexpected call.

She worked hard on Thursday. Though, on the few occasions when she did come up for air, she found that her thoughts had wandered away from her job and on to the sophisticated man she would see again tomorrow evening.

In actual fact, however, she was to see him before then. Edney went to work on Friday, brimful of enthusiasm for the new tasks she was by then absorbing more easily. And the morning went without mishap. Then, around four o'clock that afternoon, Annette was bent over her desk explaining something, when the door opened and someone came in to their office, and they both looked up.

Edney, barely remembering that she was supposed to be calm and unlikely to get in a dither, stared in amazement at the tall, dark-haired man standing there. Annette straightened. 'Saville!' she exclaimed. 'We didn't expect you until Monday!'

'I finished my business early,' he replied.

Edney's nerves had started to jump all over the place, realisation dawning as she fought to keep herself in one piece. She had thought the man who had so gently kissed her on Saturday had been away on holiday. But he hadn't! He'd been working! She started to smile—but her smile didn't quite make it. In fact, all feeling of wanting to smile froze within her as dark eyes bored icily into her. And even as she realised that she could now put a name to the man who had aided her at the party last Saturday—the man who had brought her home and had subsequently remembered her telephone number—she became startlingly aware that Saville Craythorne, her boss, the man she had a dinner date with that night, was not—if that arctic look in his eyes was anything to go by—at all pleased to see her!

CHAPTER TWO

ANNETTE swiftly introduced Edney to her employer and, while his glance skimmed over her glossy red hair and pale features, Edney saw not so much as a flicker of recognition in Saville's glance.

She opened her mouth, words teetering on her lips to say that they already knew each other. She checked herself—as it quickly dawned on her that this man did not want to know her! 'How do you do?' she forced out politely.

He inclined his head, his expression stern. But it was not to her that he addressed his remarks, but to his PA. 'If you'll come through, Annette, you can brief me on the week's happenings.'

Edney stared after them as, leading the way, Saville Craythorne strode into the adjoining office. Edney owned to feeling winded. Then pride surfaced and she started to grow angry. Who the blue blazes did he think he was? she fumed. So, okay, she got the message: he wanted to keep his business life and his social life miles apart. But not so much as a smile had he sent her way!

Bubbles to him! Mentally kicking herself that she had spent so much as a minute that week thinking about the man she had met at that party, Edney tried to get on with some work. Not so much as a smile!

Annette was still closeted with him at five o'clock. Edney had finished her work but, although there was nothing to keep her, she hesitated to go home. Then she started to get annoyed again. It crossed her mind to buzz through to the next-door office on the intercom to ask if anyone minded her going, because she'd a date that

night. She almost did, but stopped herself in time. She
wanted this job, or thought she did, and by the look of
it she was going to have to work very hard during her
trial period over the next three months, if Mr Frightened-
to-Crack-his-Face Craythorne was to approve her appointment. She didn't need to have him sack her on the
spot for impertinence. Thank heavens she didn't have to
work directly for him. Though being this close was too
close.

At twenty past five Edney checked her tidy desk, rescued her bag from its deep bottom drawer, and went
home. Saville must have worked extremely hard to be
head of the company! She had imagined the chairman
to be well past fifty.

Her father worked from home and, for him, appeared
this evening to be in a surprisingly good mood. 'Er...'
He seemed a trifle hesitant, she thought. 'Er...' he began
again. 'No need for you to cook for me tonight.'

'You're eating out?' He seldom went out in the eve-
nings.

'I ate at lunchtime. I—er—took Blanche Andrews out
to lunch,' he confessed, mentioning a widowed near-
neighbour.

Her father was taking Mrs Andrews out! She had
never known him to be remotely interested in the opposite sex since the divorce. Staring at him, Edney
glimpsed that he found his confession embarrassing, and
did what any loving daughter would do—she tried to
make light of it for him. 'I'll bet Mrs Andrews had to
pay for her own meal,' she teased.

Charles Rayner looked instantly relieved. 'I always
knew you had an impudent streak in you,' he grumbled.

It had taken meeting her new boss today to make it
surface! Now, how was she going to tell her father that
she doubted very much that she would be eating out this
evening? From Saville Craythorne's attitude at the of-

fice, she knew now that she could forget all about his promise, 'I'll call for you at seven-thirty'.

Not that she'd dream of going anyway. Clearly he wanted to keep his business and private life separate— she and he would be on two different planets, as far as she was concerned! Though, from courtesy and her well-brought-up point of view, she wished she'd thought to ask her knight errant for his phone number, the way he'd asked for hers. Or, better still, she wished she'd advised him he could save himself the trip to collect her by having taken the simple expedient of buzzing through to him on the intercom to say that it was twenty past five, but that it didn't matter, because she was breaking her date of this evening.

The phone rang. She went out into the hall and picked up the receiver. 'I can't make tonight,' he said. She knew his voice—even with the few degrees of frost it had collected since the last time she had heard it.

'Good,' she replied sweetly, and hung up. Pig! Swine! Rotter! To break their date was her prerogative. No male ever broke a date with her *ever*. How dared he? Even though she'd no intention of seeing him outside work, being stood up had never happened to her before. Her pride was once more outraged.

She went to find her father and discovered that she felt as embarrassed about telling him that she was not going out to eat as her parent had seemed to be about telling her that he already had.

'My date can't make it,' she said shortly, and caught her father's sharp look at her.

Then she realised he had somehow gleaned that she was upset. And she knew why she loved the grumbling rascal when, with mock fierceness, he quipped, 'The cad's not good enough for you!'

She laughed. 'You're right!' she grinned, adding lightly, 'Nice of him to phone.'

Nice, my best bonnet! she was fuming again when, Saville Craythorne still on her mind, she got into bed later that evening. Right, Mr Craythorne! Assuming she still had a job on Monday, from then on it was going to be strictly business. She fell asleep wishing that he would ask her for another date though—so she might have the delightful pleasure of telling him, No, thanks—you lost your chance there, sweetheart.

Edney had a busy time with her mother in Bristol on Saturday. They went shopping—her mother was tireless when it came to shopping; her shopping record was of gold medal standards.

Miles, Edney's stepbrother, of whom she was very fond, came to lunch on Sunday. Miles was tall, good-looking, twenty-six, and had moved to a flat of his own soon after his father had remarried. He and Edney met up every other Sunday when he visited his parent and stayed to lunch.

'How's the first week in your new job gone?' he asked, as the two of them pottered in the kitchen, clearing up after the meal.

Edney smiled at him. He'd remembered. 'I think I'm just beginning to see my way through the fog,' she answered.

'What's your new boss like?' Miles wanted to know.

Unspeakable—that was what he was like! 'I only met him briefly; he's been away all week.' Pride demanded that even to her superb stepbrother she could not confess that she was good enough to work in Mr Craythorne's office, but not good enough to meet him socially—for that was how it felt. 'How's your new girlfriend?' She changed the subject.

'Lettie?' He was oddly quiet for a moment, causing Edney to look at him. There was such a gentle expression on his face that she just knew Miles was in love.

'She—er—Lettie, she's—special, isn't she?' Edney questioned softly.

'You could say that,' Miles answered, and, knowing Edney would keep the information that he had a girlfriend who was special to herself, he confided, 'Lettie's extremely shy—she's not giving me much more than the fact she seems to enjoy being with me to indicate that I might be special to her.'

Edney realised that perhaps Miles felt it was too soon to ask Lettie what her feelings for him were. 'Who could help but love you?' she encouraged.

Miles grinned. 'If I manage to get her to the altar, I'll make sure you're chief bridesmaid.'

It was that serious! 'Lettie might have something to say about that,' she grinned back.

Edney was fifteen minutes into her drive back to London when thoughts of her family started mixing in with thoughts about Miles's question, 'What's your new boss like?' Somehow she was feeling decidedly restless, and wished things were different between her and Saville Craythorne. He had been so super when he'd given her a lift home from the party. She recalled his gentle kiss on her lips. That healing kiss. That...

By Monday morning, Edney was discounting that she wanted things different in any way at all. Blow Saville and his gentle kisses. 'I can't make tonight,' he'd rung to say—big of him! Oh, how she wished that she'd had his phone number so that she could have got in first. She drove to work reminding herself of Friday's promise. Strictly business. From today on, it would be strictly business.

Fat chance of it being anything else! She had thought she had worked fairly hard last week. Today, with the helmsman back, the week started with no time to so much as drink a cup of coffee. He worked her like an ox! True, he didn't spare himself either.

Not that she had a lot to do with him that Monday—her work came via Annette. Though, if he wasn't buzzing through for Annette to go in, he would come through to their office to discuss something with his PA—with not so much as a flicker of a glance in her assistant's direction.

Tuesday was as busy as Monday, and it was late in the afternoon when Annette came from Saville's office and said he wanted to see Edney. Why she should feel a sudden rush of energy in the region of her heart, Edney couldn't have said. It was, she owned, ridiculous. He was only her boss, for goodness' sake.

'Take a seat,' he instructed, not looking up when, notepad in hand, she entered his office.

Quietly, she complied, outwardly calm as she waited for him to finish what he was doing. Then he glanced up, his eyes resting momentarily on what had once been described by an admirer as her eminently kissable mouth. But not by word or look did Saville Craythorne reveal the slightest hint that his fabulous mouth had once touched hers.

Fabulous! Hurriedly Edney dragged her gaze away from his mouth. 'You wanted to see me.' She spoke first, a sudden dread hitting her that he might be about to say, Forget the three months' trial period—you're out.

But no, for all he did not look transported by her performance, it appeared that her work was up to standard when he acknowledged, 'You seem to have learned a lot in a very short time.'

High praise indeed! 'There's a lot to learn,' she answered primly.

'Which is why you won't mind working late this evening?'

Your wish is my command, O, master. 'I'd be pleased to,' she answered pleasantly—if she was going to be dismissed between now and the end of her three-month

trial period, then she wasn't about to make it easy for
him. He'd have to search jolly hard for some good rea
son to get rid of her.

He seemed to accept her answer, and went on to reveal an emergency meeting tomorrow—they cropped up
occasionally, apparently—and talked about the paperwork he wanted her to prepare for him while Annette
tackled the main body of his work for the following
morning.

Managing to keep her expression composed, Edney
left his office with her head full of this file, that file, note
this and don't forget that—on pain of your life, don't
forget the other! She got down to work.

It was six o'clock before she remembered she had a
father at home waiting to be fed—and she might not
have remembered then had she not overheard Annette
on the phone to her elderly mother, with whom she
lived, to let her know she was going to be late.

Edney followed suit, and, taking up the phone, dialled
her home number. 'It's me,' she announced, and, finding
she had the office to herself while Annette was next
door, she suggested, 'I don't suppose you'd like to take
Mrs Andrews out to dinner—my treat?'

'You're working late?' He was clever, her father.

'It's all happening here,' she replied.

'Bring some chips in.'

The next time she surfaced, it was seven o'clock.
Annette was back and took a breather at about the same
time. 'We haven't put you off, have we?' she asked a
shade anxiously.

'Not at all,' Edney answered; she'd truly enjoyed having to be on her toes. She felt alive, eager to learn, and
found the work inspiring—this week particularly so.

It had rained all day, and was still raining when, about
forty minutes later they had all the paperwork ready for
the next day and everything locked away. The three of

them left the office together, and Edney was suddenly very conscious of Saville Craythorne standing next to her in the lift.

She was slender, and five feet eight—but he, athletic, lean and muscular, still towered over her. She was having trouble with her breathing. Funny, she'd never suffered from claustrophobia before!

Edney was first out of the lift and first out of the building as they made for the car park. 'Goodnight, Annette. Goodnight, Sav... Mr Craythorne,' she hastily corrected, and was never more glad that she had parked her car some way away from theirs.

Oh, help, she'd almost called him by his first name! Half had, she realised, and knew it was because she was so used to hearing Annette refer to him as Saville. It had just sort of slipped out. Partly from embarrassment at her gaffe—he'd made it plain he didn't want her being anywhere near *that* personal—slapped wrists, remember he's the chairman!—and partly because of the pouring rain, Edney hastened to unlock the driver's door of her Mini.

Intending to be first out of the car park, she lost valuable seconds when her car keys decided, that night of all nights, to be elusive. And, when she had finally harvested them from the bottom of her bag, was seat-belted and had her key in the ignition, Annette was already on the move.

Edney smiled and waved to Annette as she passed, and found a second to wonder why she was panicking. Heavens, getting into a lather just because she had almost called that arrogant swine by his first name!

Making herself calm down, Edney turned the key in the ignition—the Mini did not respond. She tried again—nothing. She couldn't believe it—her Mini was such a reliable little vehicle, it had *never* let her down!

She tried again, and kept on trying. Not so much as a spark could get out of the engine.

She glanced up—that was all she needed; Saville Craythorne had pulled up within speaking distance. Despite the teeming rain, he had his window down and was indicating that she open hers too.

Who was she to disobey? She opened her window. 'It won't start.' She stated the obvious—and, cutting his question off before he could ask it, she continued, 'it's never done this before.'

He gave an impatient glance at his watch. 'I'd better give you a lift home,' he decided shortly.

She'd sooner walk! 'No need. I can call out a mechanic and...'

'Stop arguing,' he commanded—just asking for a punch on the nose. 'Lock your car up and get into mine.'

'I'll get a taxi home,' she informed him; to hell with the expense—she'd be damned if she'd allow him to rescue her a second time!

'Confound it, woman!' Saville Craythorne exploded suddenly. 'I've got something better to do with my evening than to sit in a car park arguing with you! Come and get in!'

Oh, so the great man had some female waiting for him to call! Edney experienced the most odd, unpleasant sensation—every bit as though she found the thought of him with a close woman-friend upsetting. What tosh!

Reluctantly, though swiftly, since she did not welcome a soaking, Edney exited her Mini, locked it and quickly occupied the seat in Saville's car she had used— grief, was it only ten days ago?

For the first five minutes of the journey she quietly fumed against the bossy brute. She'd no wish to cut into the time he spent with his woman-friend. Then Edney started to wonder where her brain had gone—had she been thinking at all clearly, she would have thought to tell the brute that her father would come out for her. She could have rung him. He'd have grumbled, of course— as he would when he knew he was driving her to work in the morning—but he would have come and collected her.

Gradually her annoyance with Saville Craythorne— okay, so he was doing her a favour, but he could have been less impatient about it—started to wane. She even found that she was giving him a few Brownie points since, though he could easily have left her stranded, he had not. True, it was because of working late for him that there was no one else around to help her at that time of night—as it was true, for all her proud protestation, 'I can call a mechanic', that she hadn't a clue which garage might still be open and have someone prepared to come out on such a foul night.

Edney started to relax. So, all right, her employer was not saying a word, but for some reason she didn't feel the silence was oppressive. If she believed, however, that the rest of the drive to her home was to be completed in silence, she discovered herself mistaken.

'It's early days yet, but are you enjoying your work this far?' Saville Craythorne, his earlier impatience seemingly forgotten, put himself out to ask.

Edney had an idea that her employer wouldn't bother looking for an excuse if he wanted her out, but never- theless she was on her guard not to supply him with ammunition which might backfire on her later.

Although, in this instance, she didn't really have to think about it, and was totally honest when she replied, 'I'm loving it. I find the work I'm doing so far extremely interesting and challenging.'

He didn't say, Good. He didn't smile. In fact, she had no idea how he reacted to her answer. But at least he didn't say, Tough, either. They drove the rest of the way in silence. For all that he had been to her home only once before, and had come from a different direction then, Saville Craythorne drove straight there now, not needing any help in finding his way.

They were going up the drive to her home before she remembered she was supposed to bring some fish and chips home. She checked her watch as Saville drew the car to a standstill, wondering if she wanted to get her father's car out and make the four-mile journey to the chip shop before it closed.

'Date?'

Edney, her hand on the door handle, turned sideways to realise that her employer had spotted her checking her watch and was asking if she had a date that night. She didn't—but there was no need to tell him that.

'Thanks to you, I'll just make it,' she replied, and smiled. He didn't, but more scowled instead she rather thought. Edney decided to make herself scarce. 'Goodnight,' she said, adding, 'And—er—thank you,' and swiftly got out of there. If he answered her goodnight, she didn't hear it. What she did hear was his sleek and elegant car departing—he was obviously keen to start his evening's pleasure.

Strangely she could not get thoughts of Saville Craythorne out of her head when she went to bed that night. Was he home yet? Or was he, for want of better words, still out wining and dining?

She awoke to a sunny day, unbelievable after yesterday's non-stop rain, and went downstairs to find that her father was up and had condescended to boil a kettle. 'You'd better ring me if you want a lift home as well as to work,' he surprised her by offering.

'I hope I'll be able to get the Mini fixed and won't have to trouble you—but it's sweet of you to offer.'

'Sweet?' he questioned—nobody had ever accused him of being *sweet* before. 'I just thought you wouldn't want to bother your Mr Craythorne two nights running.'

She very much doubted 'her Mr Craythorne' would *offer* two nights running. It was more probable he would think her grossly inefficient to have to need his help yet again.

Her father got her to work in plenty of time to start her business day, and, because she was early, he parked his car and went with her to the Mini. 'Get in and give her a try,' he suggested.

It seemed pointless to Edney, but in the past he had always managed to find an answer to her problems. But, given that he was more inclined to do any minor repairs to his own car, rather than pay what he termed 'over the odds' to let some garage do them, perhaps he thought it was some simple fault he could fix in a few minutes himself.

Taking her keys, she unlocked the car and did as her father had bidden. She turned the key in the ignition—and looked at her father incredulously when it behaved perfectly and started at once.

'I couldn't get a peep out of it last night!' she protested. 'No matter how I tried I couldn't. How...?'

'Quite simple,' her father replied smugly. 'The plugs and points must have got soaked in yesterday's downpour—and a kind wind overnight dried them out again.' He went on his way the happiest she'd seen him for a while, and she went into the I. L. building thinking that she would park her car in a more sheltered spot from tomorrow onwards.

She saw nothing of Saville Craythorne that morning, and very little of his PA, who went with him to take minutes of the emergency meeting.

Thrown in at the deep end, as it were, Edney felt pleased that she coped as she fielded telephone calls, making exact notes of every one, and generally held the fort until lunchtime.

At one o'clock she took all her notes into Saville

Craythorne's office and left them neatly on his desk, and then took herself off for a sandwich and a cup of coffee and, later, to quickly shop in the local supermarket for that evening's meal.

It was as she was waiting at the check-out that she bumped into a friend of her stepbrother's whom she hadn't seen for years. 'Edney...!' he exclaimed, recognising her straight away.

'Rayner,' she supplied, and smiled. She had always liked him then, he had been friendly without being familiar. 'Graeme—Jowett,' she pulled out of her memory-file.

'How long is it? You were about sixteen. Stunning then—sensational now.' But, finding that queuing and paying was not conducive to conversation, he asked, 'Have you time for a drink?'

She shook her head. 'I must get back to the office.'

'Are you free for dinner tonight? We could catch up,' he suggested.

There were several good reasons why she should not accept his mid-week invitation. Tomorrow was another day at the office—late nights were not calculated to have her bright-eyed and bushy-tailed for work in the morning. Added to that, she would prefer to give her father more warning.

'I'm sorry, I...'

'You're not married or anything?'

'No,' she smiled. 'You?'

'Recovering from a rather bruising divorce,' he owned openly. Going on swiftly, as though his divorce was still extremely painful to him, he asked, 'So, if you're not free tonight, how about tomorrow or Friday?'

He was a very pleasant man, was Graeme. As unbidden thoughts of Saville Craythorne came into her head—he'd been out on the town last night, regardless that he'd got a heavy meeting today—so, too, did an unknown rebellious streak in her nature suddenly materialise. Hang it, she was twenty-two! If she couldn't take just one late night in her stride, then she considered it a very poor show.

'I'd love to dine with you tomorrow,' she accepted, and returned to her office. Graeme had insisted he would call for her, and he'd mentioned one of the most exclusive restaurants where they would dine.

Annette was extremely busy after that morning's meeting, and if she hadn't seen it before Edney was now very much aware of why the PA needed an assistant. They were both hard at work when just after four Saville Craythorne came into their office from the corridor. He had another man with him, a fair-haired man who was a few inches shorter than he, but still tall; he was somewhere in his late twenties, Edney guessed.

Saville Craythorne glanced her way and, without a word, went over to discuss some complicated issue with Annette. His companion, clearly liking what he saw, lingered at Edney's desk.

'What happened to Pippa?' he asked, laying on charm by the barrowload. 'No, don't tell me! Just tell me who you are and why my cousin has been keeping you such a dark secret?'

Edney opened her mouth, ready with a reply of sorts—but discovered that her employer was not so engrossed with the discussion he was having with Annette as she had thought.

'Miss Rayner has only just started with us, and is much too busy learning her job to have time to waste,' Saville Craythorne cut in shortly.

Edney closed her mouth, feeling that she was the one who'd been put in her place rather than his cousin. That newborn rebellion surged again—for crying out loud, she'd done nothing wrong! She'd been quietly minding her own business until they'd come in.

'Edney Rayner,' she introduced herself, extending her right hand to the cousin. From Saville's tone just now, she deduced he planned to get rid of her between now and the end of her three-month trial, so what the blazes?

The cousin beamed a grin from ear to ear. 'Welcome to the firm, Edney.' He, at any rate, seemed pleased that she was working there. 'Felix Stevens.' He returned the introduction, taking her right hand in his and making a thorough job of it. 'Cousin, director, and appreciator of beauty.'

Edney was about to retrieve her hand, the better to get on with some work, when Saville rescued her verbally. 'I rather think Edney needs both hands for that paper she's typing!' he informed his cousin. Edney! We're coming on! 'We'll go to my office.'

Reluctantly, Felix Stevens let go of her hand. 'I shall return,' he said softly.

All too obviously he was a dreadful flirt, though Edney managed to wait until he and Saville had gone through to the other office and closed the door before she gave a small laugh. 'Is he always like that?' she asked Annette.

'Always,' Annette confirmed.

Funnily enough, Edney went home that night in a lighter mood than of late. True, she still wasn't Saville Craythorne's most favourite person, but at least she'd met two men today who thought she was worthy of a second look. So, sucks boo to Saville Craythorne—who wanted to be his favourite person anyway?

Edney and Annette were still working under pressure the next day, and she kept her head down when, once in the morning and twice during the afternoon, Saville, instead of sending for Annette, strode through to consult her about some business matter.

At the end of that day Edney dashed home, and was changed and ready when Graeme arrived. Her father approved. With his blessing, she and Graeme went out to his smart up-to-the-minute car. During the journey she learned that Graeme worked in connection with the stock market. Because everything about him spoke money, she realised that she need not worry that their dinner was going to cost more than he could afford.

He was good company, though she knew at once that he was never going to set her world on fire. She had never been to that particular restaurant before, but she felt quite relaxed as she and Graeme chatted through the meal.

The more they chatted, the more comfortable Edney felt with Graeme; comfortable and totally unthreatened. 'Ever visit Bristol these days?' she asked as they were sipping coffee.

'I must, I must,' he said, and added, more to himself than to her, 'I was happy there.'

And a look of such bleak unhappiness crossed his expression that she realised that he was still very much in love with his ex-wife. Instinctively she stretched out across the table in a gesture of sympathy.

His hand gripped hers and she quickly glanced away to give him a chance to recover. Then promptly, in glancing away, she looked up—and wished she hadn't. Saville Craythorne! He had appeared out of nowhere! He had seen her, and his ice-cold inspection was flicking from her wide blue eyes to the way she and her escort were holding hands across the table.

In that initial, fleeting moment her brain seemed to seize up, and all she could think was that the man she worked for would assume she had a hand-holding fettish: first his cousin's and now someone else's.

Then that part of her that was calm and unlikely to get in a dither kicked in, and, albeit that her insides were chasing around like nobody's business, she managed to ignore the impulse to snatch her hand away from

Graeme's. She was glad she had when her line of vision widened and she took note of the quite stunning brunette her employer was escorting.

'Sorry to be wet!' Graeme apologised, reminding her where she was.

Dragging her gaze from her good-looking employer—goodness, did he have it all!—Edney smiled at Graeme and, since she was convinced Saville was not going to acknowledge her as he passed by, did her utmost to pretend that her nerve-ends were not aquiver at seeing him so unexpectedly.

Unfortunately some compulsion, some magnetic force, made her look up again—just as Saville and his companion drew level with their table. Wide blue eyes met cool dark eyes full on. They were not friendly dark eyes.

But there was nothing wrong with his manners; she had to give him that. 'Good evening,' he acknowledged her.

'Hello,' she answered, and, the moment over as he and his woman-friend continued on to their table, Edney wanted to go home. She felt all churned up inside, all of a tremble, and, while she would like to pretend that Saville Craythorne had no effect on her whatsoever, she was beginning to realise that she *was* very much affected by the cold-eyed, unfriendly monster!

CHAPTER THREE

BY MORNING Edney was contradicting that she was in any way affected by her employer, other than being concerned that she wouldn't last her three-month trial period if he had anything to do with it.

She drove to her office, reliving last night again while honestly acknowledging that, yes, she had felt all upset in the region of her tummy. But that had only been because she had seen Saville Craythorne in the restaurant so unexpectedly. She found it a bitter pill to swallow that she had to see him outside the office as well as in.

It had been a surprise that he had deigned to offer that 'Good evening', though, and she admitted that she was being unfair if she believed it was beneath him to acknowledge anyone as lowly as an assistant PA.

She decided not to think about him, but found she was wondering about his stunning brunette companion instead. She didn't want to think of her either, so she ousted the brunette from her mind and concentrated her thoughts on Graeme.

Again, after taking her home, he had proved what a very nice man he was when he'd attempted to kiss her before she went in and had taken her refusal '...if you don't mind I'd rather we weren't that sort of kissing friends...' as she'd hoped, even to the extent of seeming a little relieved when, apologising, he had said, 'Sorry, I thought it was expected of me.' From that she gathered that the only person he ever wanted to kiss was his ex-wife, Lindy. 'Will you show you hold no hard feelings by coming to a party with me on Saturday? I'm expected to go—I work with James—only if I don't take someone,

I just know he and Laura will have somebody "suitable" lined up for me.'

'I'd love to come,' she'd accepted.

Friday was as busy as every other day so far, but, the work becoming much more clear to her now, Edney began to think that she might, just might, be able to cope when Annette took her annual holiday in two weeks' time.

Saville came into the office she shared with Annette around midday. Edney, hearing his door start to open, kept her eyes absorbed in the matter she was working on. She felt all fluttery inside, and while he took some paperwork to Annette's desk, Edney, her fingers suddenly all thumbs on her keyboard, was glad when the phone rang. Since Annette was obviously busy, Edney took the call.

'Mr Craythorne's office.'

'Ah, that can be none other than the delectable Edney!'

She knew the manner, even if she wasn't quite sure of the voice. 'Mr Stevens?' she queried, and, absently flicking her gaze upwards, saw that at the mention of his cousin's name Saville, as if expecting the call would be for him, was giving her his attention.

The problem was that with both her employer and his PA stopping what they were doing, Edney realised she now had a very attentive audience for what, she was soon made aware, was not a business call at all.

'The very same,' Felix Stevens answered, 'but I shall be devastated if you don't call me Felix.'

'I...' she began.

'Go on, say it, say my name.'

She was starting to feel a little pink about the ears, and quite desperately wanted this call to end—while at the same time being very much aware that her telephone

manner might be on trial here. 'Felix,' she complied, as
pleasantly as she was able, feeling a fool.

'Music,' he murmured—and she started to grow a little irritated, confused and, on account of her listeners,
pink-cheeked as well as pink-eared.

By the sound of it, Felix Stevens had time to talk all
day; there was nothing for it but, director of the firm or
not, to hurry him on. 'Mr Craythorne is in my office
now if you wish to speak…'

'Lord, no. It's you I rang to speak to,' he replied in-
timately.

'Oh,' she said, desperately trying to keep her telephone manner. She'd got work to do. 'You need my help
in some way?'

'Now there's a leading question,' he answered, but
then he came to the point. 'Come out with me tomorrow?' he asked. 'I know a…'

'I'm sorry, Mr Stev… Felix, I have a date tomorrow
and…'

'I knew it!' he exclaimed, but recovered to ask, 'How
about Sunday? We could…'

'I'm sorry,' she began, only Felix was still talking.

Then all of a sudden he wasn't. And neither was the
phone in her hand any longer because, impatiently, without so much as a May I?, Saville had taken the receiver
from her, told his cousin, 'Goodbye, Felix,' and
slammed it down on its rest. While Edney looked at him
in amazement, he stared down at her and, his expression
grim, barked, 'Any objections?'

Oh, grief, she was going to laugh. 'Er—not one,' she
managed, and when she saw his glance go down to her
upward-turning mouth—and stay there—she just knew
that her lips were twitching.

Then, while she was wondering if to laugh at one's
boss was a sackable offence, she saw, unbelievably, the
corners of his mouth start to twitch too. He thought it

amusing as well. Incredibly, they shared the same sense
of humour!

His smile, however, did not make it. Their eyes met
briefly, then he was turning from her. 'Annette,' he said,
and returned to his office. Annette followed.

A busy afternoon was spent, with Annette clearing her
desk early because she was taking her mother to a medi-
cal appointment. Left in the office by herself after
Annette had gone, Edney was very much aware of the
man in the next-door office.

At five she started to tidy up, while wondering at the
same time if she should go and say goodnight to him or
just leave. The fact that it appeared he could, without
remotely trying, make her laugh had softened her attitude towards him, she had to own.

At ten past five she took her bag from her drawer and
put it on the top of her desk. Then she straightened and
almost put it back again when the door between the two
offices opened. Saville, his expression stern, spotted at
once her bag sitting on her otherwise clear desk.

'About to leave?' he queried shortly.

'I can stay if…' she began to offer.

He shook his head. 'There's nothing that can't wait
until Monday.' And, almost in the same breath, he surprised her by asking, 'Get your car fixed?'

From his stern look she knew he'd just love it if she
asked him for a lift home. 'It wasn't broken,' she replied.
'My father brought me in on Wednesday. According to
him, the plugs and points had got soaked in Tuesday's
downpour and dried out overnight.' Grief, she sounded
boring! 'Well, I'll be off,' she added hurriedly—but saw
his dark eyes were scrutinising her face.

'You look tired!' he observed abruptly.

Well, thanks! She'd worked like a slave that day! 'I'll
get over it,' she responded as evenly as she could, and
picked up her bag.

'You want to get to bed early at night!' he rapped.

Dash it, who the Dickens did he think he was? She and Graeme had been drinking their coffee last night before *he'd* so much as ordered his starter! 'I did!' she snapped—and only as his face set like granite did she realise he had misconstrued her answer. She had meant only to hint that, in relation to the hours he kept, she had gone to bed very early. But, from the filthy look that accompanied his granite expression, she at once knew he had taken her hint to mean that she had gone to bed early—with the man she had been out with!

He was back in his office with the door firmly shut by the time she'd worked that out. Oh, great, not only had she snapped at him—this man who held her professional fate in his hands—but, contrary to the truth, he now thought her not averse to rounding off a pleasant dinner with bedtime for two. Not that it was any of his business!

But so much for thinking they shared the same sense of humour. There hadn't been much humour showing on that granite face. She went to the outer door—he could whistle if he thought she was going into his office to say she was off and to wish him a nice weekend! Edney drove home, oddly unsure whether she was glad or sorry that she wouldn't see Saville Craythorne again before Monday.

The party with Graeme on Saturday was enjoyable, and the week ended on a pleasant note. Feeling refreshed, Edney started the following week feeling she was really getting to grips with her job. But, for all that her employer came into her office from time to time, she had very little to do with him.

Annette was in Saville's office on Friday morning, with the door closed, when the outer office door opened and Felix Stevens came in. He looked delighted to see Edney—and she feared the worst. Had he wanted a word with his cousin, then surely he would have gone in to see him using the other door which opened straight from the corridor into Saville's office.

'With difficulty,' he began, 'I've left it a whole week before asking you out again.'

'I'm—er—busy this evening,' she was able to tell him—thank you, Graeme! He was calling for her at eight.

Felix was not to be put off. Though, unfortunately, his suggestion, 'How about tomorrow—you must let me take you to dinner tomorrow,' coincided with the door between the two offices opening and Annette coming through. 'Morning, Annette. You're a clever lady; tell me what I have to do to get your delightful assistant to come out with me.'

'You're on your own,' Annette replied pleasantly, letting him know politely she had no intention of being drawn into the conversation.

Annette was about to close the door to Saville's office when she noticed, as had Edney who was just wanting to die, that Saville had come to stand there. 'Got a problem, Felix?' he questioned.

'Not now that Edney has just agreed to have dinner with me tomorrow.'

Edney's eyes widened. 'Actually, I haven't.' She got in there fast. Thank goodness for Bristol. 'I'm sorry, Felix, I'm going away for the weekend.' Overnight on Saturday, anyway.

He looked crestfallen, comically crestfallen, so much so that she almost laughed. One glance at Saville's murderous expression put paid to that, though. *Now* what had she done?

'We're busy,' Saville grunted. And, when his cousin didn't take the hint, by the simple expedient of removing the centre of his attention, Saville did away with any need for Felix to linger. 'Come into my office, Edney,' he instructed, and turned about, clearly expecting her to jump to his bidding.

Edney got to her feet. She'd done nothing wrong, but by the look of it she was about to be well and truly carpeted. It infuriated her, embarrassed her that in front of the other two, Saville should make it so obvious that he was displeased with her. She gave serious thought to going in the other direction—all the way home.

Annette saved the day, salving Edney's embarrassment by stating in an undertone, 'You'll need your pad. Saville suggested it might be the right moment to see what you're made of.'

Thus challenged, though still angry, Edney managed a half-smile to Annette and also one in Felix's direction. Picking up a pad and pencil, she went quickly after her employer.

He was standing, icy-eyed, waiting for her when she went into his office—and she guessed she could forget all about note-taking. 'What did I do?' she asked coldly, in no mood just then to meekly take her dismissal.

His answer was to walk around her and close the door. Edney got the picture—so it wasn't to be a public dismissal, then. Her mother had blamed her red hair for her sometimes fiery temperament. But for the most part Edney had always managed to control her temper. But this—this injustice—was more than she could bear calmly.

'My stars!' she flared when, still without a word, Saville, who wasn't intending to sit for this interview, apparently, returned to stand behind his desk. 'To think I was too shy to tell you where I was starting work in case you thought I was showing off!'

He seemed a degree surprised, as much by what she said as by her reference to their first meeting. But Edney knew he'd be telling her she was leaving any minute now. She opened her mouth, ready to tell him what she thought of that—then found that she was the one who was surprised, when he more snarled than questioned. 'You're trying to make me believe that you didn't know who I was that night of Jeremy Knowles's party?'

Startled, she stared at him. He couldn't, all this while, have believed that she'd known who he was—even while she was telling him that she was between jobs? That he was her new boss? 'Of course I didn't know!' she got her breath back to retort. If she was getting slung out on her ear—and there didn't seem much doubt about that—then she'd be hanged if she was going quietly. 'How *would* I know? Nobody introduced us!'

'You checked me out!' he reminded her curtly. 'I particularly asked you if...'

'I only checked—bearing in mind I'd just had to fight off Tony Watson—if you were safe—er—in that department!' Her anger was fading—she wanted it back. 'But I didn't know your name—who you were. Goodness!' she gasped, 'You haven't gone around all this time thinking that I knew you were my new employer?'

'What I think or thought then is no longer relevant.' He cut her off, bluntly letting her know that while he once might have felt inclined to invite her out—during a phone call from Milan no less—that was no longer the case. She didn't thank him for that either. 'What I'm more interested in is the smooth running of my office— which is not helped when it is constantly interrupted while you deal with your love life.'

'Love life!' Her anger was back; she was glad of it. 'He's *your* cousin!' she erupted. 'Tell *him*, not me!' She just wasn't going to take this! To hear him tell it, the phone never ceased ringing and men beat a constant path to her office door. 'Twice!' she stormed on, 'just twice has Felix Stevens asked me out. And twice I've turned him down!' With her blue eyes sparking with feelings

of hostility, Edney glared at her employer—ex-employer
any minute now, if she was any judge! 'All I ever
wanted when I came to work here was a job I could get
my teeth into. A job that was stimulating.' Why the
blazes should she go out with a whimper? 'I wanted this
job, and I thought I was getting good at it,' she ranted
on. She paused for breath—and then found her breath
was very nearly taken away when, his look no less hostile, Saville Craythorne cut in.

'Then sit down and let's see just how good you really
are,' he suggested curtly.

For all of three seconds Edney stared at him, open-
mouthed. He wasn't dismissing her! He hadn't called her
in to say, On your way! He really did want her to take
notes! There was a seat near his desk—Edney took it
before her legs gave way. And then started to learn
something else—the man was a machine, an automaton.
She had been given work by him once before and had
thought that tough. But this! For the next hour, without
pause or falter, Saville instructed and her fingers flew
over her notepad.

At the end of that hour, her head was full of a hundred
and one things: type back, discover, ring here, ring there,
cancel this. So, if she had ever been angry and had heatedly fired off a few rounds at her employer, she had no
recollection just then of why.

'Is that all?' she asked when he finally came to a full
stop. All? Any more and she'd be on her *knees*!

'For the moment,' Saville agreed, so pleasantly that
Edney started to feel certain that he had thrown everything at her on purpose.

'How did I do?' His pleasant manner made her brave
enough to ask.

His lips twitched—she was sure of it. But he was short
on praise as he drawled, 'I'll let you know when I see

the finished results.' She stood up and, her head swimming, went calmly from his office.

In her own office, the communicating door closed, Edney collapsed onto her chair. 'Tough?' Annette enquired sympathetically.

'Tell me it doesn't get any worse, *please*!' Edney begged.

She was still feeling a little fragile, her brain used up, when she went out with Graeme that night, so she was glad he was the uncomplicated person he was. She didn't think she could cope with complicated that night.

She had recovered by the time she drove to Bristol the next day, and was able to tell her stepbrother on Sunday that she had bumped into Graeme and how he was faring. But, for all she had spent an enjoyable enough time in Bristol, she realised she was glad to be going back to London.

And, at the start of another new week, she found that she was feeling excited inside, and really looking forward to going to work. That, though, was before she actually entered her office. Unusually, Saville's door was open, and she could see him at his desk as she neared her own. She also saw he was looking in her direction— perhaps roused by the sound of the outer door opening— and crazily her heart started to hurry in its beating.

'Good morning,' she offered, quickly turning from his unsmiling expression to include Annette in her greeting.

'Nice weekend?' Annette asked with a smile, acquainted by then with the fact that Edney visited her mother in Bristol on alternate weekends.

'Very enjoyable,' she replied, and, somehow unable to resist a glance back to Saville, she was startled when—clearly not liking his concentration interrupted by her prattle, and looking extremely displeased— Saville left his desk and, with a determined thud, closed the door, shutting her and her voice out.

Not a very auspicious start to the week, Edney felt, but with Annette due to go on holiday on Friday evening for two weeks, the next few days seemed to fly by as Edney soaked up all instruction.

Felix Stevens asked her again for a date. She was getting to quite like Felix, but she was grateful that Saville wasn't around at the time; it seemed to irk him that she wasted his office time dealing with what he termed her 'love life'. Nonetheless, Edney again turned Felix down.

Friday appeared before she was ready for it. 'You'll cope; I know you will.' Annette smiled, sounding far more confident than Edney was suddenly starting to feel. 'And don't forget if you do need any help, which I'm sure you won't, Pippa is only along the corridor.'

Edney felt it was a point of honour that she should cope without needing to call on Pippa. At five that evening she warmly wished Annette a super holiday—and went home knowing that, come Sunday evening, she was going to go to bed early in order to be alert and ready for anything Saville Craythorne threw at her.

On Saturday she went out with Graeme—but found she spent a lot of time thinking of Saville. Edney pulled herself together, deciding that the pressure of knowing it would be just her and him next week was getting to her.

She was wearing a new long-skirted charcoal suit teamed with a green shirt when she went into the office on Monday. Her red hair was shining; what little make-up she wore was perfect. She had taken pains with her appearance. She was inwardly extremely anxious and needed to feel good.

Saville was there before her—he always was, so Lord knew what time he'd arrived at the office. 'Good morning, Mr Craythorne,' she offered as she went in. His office door was open again this Monday.

'Didn't I hear you refer to me by my first name last Friday?' he enquired, stopping her dead in her tracks.

Yes, he had. She and Annette had been in conversation about work and she'd said, 'Would Saville want more than one copy?' or something of the sort. She hadn't known he'd overheard, though!

'Er—did you mind?' she asked tentatively, fearing the next fortnight was going to be all uphill before it got started.

'Not if you don't mind my calling you Edney,' he replied evenly. And suddenly it was a lovely, lovely day. For surely he had just invited her to call him by his first name.

She worked extremely hard that first week of Annette's absence, and, while admitting she was fully stretched, Edney drove home at the end of it realising that never had she enjoyed a week so much.

Edney invited Graeme to meet some of her friends on Saturday, and spent Sunday mentally recharging her batteries. When she went into her office on Monday she was ready and eager to start her second week as acting PA to Saville Craythorne. His door was open when she went in. 'Good morning, Saville,' she greeted him brightly.

'You sound as though you had a good weekend.'

An average weekend by anybody's standards. 'I did,' she answered enthusiastically.

He didn't answer her smile, but questioned curtly, 'I expect you went away again?'

Pardon her for breathing! Now what was the matter? 'I went out with some friends,' she replied evenly—only he was taking up some paperwork; clearly he wasn't interested.

Monday was difficult, but there was an improvement on Tuesday. And first thing on Wednesday morning Saville called her into his office to tell her that unexpectedly he was flying to Frankfurt tomorrow morning. He instructed her to cancel his Thursday and Friday appointments and, looking up sharply, added, 'You'll have to handle things on your own for the next couple of days.'

There was a query there. 'No problem.' She answered his unvoiced, Are you up to it? calmly, and hoped that she was the only one who knew that she was inwardly quailing. On her *own*! Oh, Mother!

'Good!' He accepted her word, and proceeded to give her lengthy instructions, ending by saying, 'I'm afraid we're going to have to work quite late tonight.' Considerately, she thought, he added, 'Is there anyone you have to call? Some boyfriend...?'

'My father,' she responded. 'I'd better tell him to make some other arrangements for his meal.'

Unexpectedly Saville smiled. It lightened his face and, her heart giving a little jump, Edney stared at him. He cared not, it seemed, that her father would be trotting off to the fish and chip shop. She smiled too—then went swiftly to her own office.

'I'm going to be very late tonight,' she informed her father when she rang him. 'Can you get yourself something to eat?'

'I've been giving thought to asking Blanche Andrews out to dinner—perhaps tonight would be a good time,' he answered. 'Are you getting paid overtime?'

He really was an old rascal. Just as he knew that she couldn't discuss such matters on the phone when her employer might be in earshot, he also knew that she was extremely well paid.

'Goodbye, Father,' she said, unconsciously borrowing Saville's manner from the occasion when he had terminated Felix's call to her. She heard her father's wicked chuckle before he put down his phone.

It was work, work, work from then on. Although

when, at half past one, Saville came from his office to place some paperwork on her desk and found her still working there he ordered her to go and have something to eat.

'I'll just finish this,' she answered.

'Now,' he said firmly.

'But...' she began to protest, changed her mind when she saw he was insisting that she did as he said—and suddenly, she smiled. 'Shall I bring you back a sandwich?' she asked prettily.

He stared at her innocent eyes, his glance going down to her sweetly upward-curving mouth. 'My G...' he began, and changed whatever he had been about to say to, 'Yes, to that sandwich, and, for your sauce, you can brew some fresh coffee when you get back.'

Sauce! Edney, still smiling, feeling good inside, went to obey his orders. She was back at two, though, and, after taking him his sandwich she went to the corner of the room where a hotplate and coffee-making equipment stood, and made him a drink.

Feeling refreshed, and eager to carry on from where she left off, Edney returned to her own desk. Then time simply flew. She didn't see three o'clock, nor four. But at half past four, and bearing a cup of tea, Saville came in to see her.

He handed her the tea, and she owned to feeling inordinately pleased by his simple action. The last time she had seen him he had been totally absorbed in what he was doing. That he should remember her too, when at last taking a breather, was quite uplifting.

'Why, thank you,' she said, deciding, since he was still standing there, to take a breather too. She leaned back in her chair and, looking at him, suddenly found she was wishing things were different—that he had not cancelled their date, and that she had the chance to know him as a man, not just as her employer.

He looked down at her for a few moments, his dark eyes taking in her creamy skin, though what he was thinking she had no idea. Then abruptly he was referring to the papers on her desk. 'How are things going?' he asked.

'ETF around seven-thirty,' she returned.

'ETF?'

'Estimated time of finishing—and with a following wind,' she explained—and it was head down, hard at it again.

It was ten past seven when Edney took the last of what she had been doing into the next-door office. 'That was some following wind,' Saville remarked, checking his watch. Decisive as always, he continued, 'There are still a few matters I need to discuss with you. Tidy your desk and we'll discuss issues that may arise over dinner.'

Edney felt her cheeks grow hot. 'Right,' she answered, and turned swiftly about. Grief, it was only logical that they ate—she mustn't read anything into it that wasn't there! She was starving, he was starving—and there was still a lot he needed to instruct her about, apparently. What could be more logical than they should satisfy hunger pangs while they completed discussing everything that still had to be covered? For her part, she'd be happy to talk until midnight, if it meant she would be able to run his office more efficiently in his absence.

They left the building together, but then Saville gave her the name of the restaurant and they travelled there in their own cars. It was a pleasant venue, one she had not been to before. And, she realised, Saville must have telephoned in advance. They were expected, and, because of the business they would discuss, Saville had requested an alcove table.

'I've not been here before,' Edney saw no harm in

remarking, as she made her choice from the menu and looked about.

'Have you not?' he remarked conversationally, and teasingly he continued, 'Not one of the group you go around with has thought to bring you here?'

She rather thought she enjoyed his teasing. She was delighted, too, that he had remembered from that night of their first meeting that she had told him she had a group of friends she went around with—delighted that he should mention something personal.

Though, no sooner had their first course arrived, it was business all the way—right through to the pudding course. 'That's about it, I think,' Saville stated, as she tried to remember everything he'd said. 'Coffee?'

Somehow, though this was a business dinner and nothing more, she was not ready for the evening to end. 'I'd love some,' she accepted. 'That was a super meal,' she saw no harm in mentioning—her trout with almonds had been something else again.

'You normally cook for yourself and your father?' Saville questioned.

Edney recalled mentioning that morning she'd have to let her father know to make other arrangements for his meal that night. 'Normally,' she agreed. 'Though tonight my father said he'd ask a neighbour he's friendly with if she'd like to have dinner with him somewhere.'

'You don't mind that he has a lady-friend?' Saville startled her by asking.

Their coffee arrived, giving her a moment in which to think about it. She wasn't sure Mrs Andrews could be termed 'lady-friend', but, on reflection, she answered, 'I want him to be happy. Though he can be a bit crusty sometimes, so I wouldn't want him to rush anything— not that he's showing any signs of rushing.' She smiled. But, suddenly feeling that she was showing her father up in a poor light, she added quickly, 'He's a wonderful

father,' tacking on too quickly in her need to show what
a wonderful parent she had, 'He wanted to write to you,
by the way, er...' she broke off—oh, no, her tongue!
She was getting herself into much too deep water!

Naturally Saville Craythorne didn't leave it there; she
somehow hadn't thought he would. 'He did?' he queried.

There was nothing for it. Inwardly squirming, she felt
forced to reveal, 'When I told him how you'd rescued
me from Tony Watson he—when he'd got over wanting
to go and flatten Tony—he wanted to write and thank
you for bringing me home.'

Still squirming, Edney found her coffee cup of great
interest, and only looked up when, that teasing note there
again, Saville probed, 'Do you tell your father everything, Edney?'

She smiled. She loved his teasing. 'Absolutely,' she
answered, 'He might be a bit crusty at times, but I've
always been able to talk to him about everything, tell
him everything. Oh...' She suddenly broke off, and then
had to confess, 'Only, come to think of it, I've never
told him that you and the man he called—um...' She
wished she hadn't got started on this.

'I'm intrigued?' Saville prompted.

She didn't want to continue. She wanted to hide under
the table, to go home, but Saville was still waiting. 'He
called you my—knight in shining armour,' she said
quickly, not looking at him but rushing on. 'Anyhow, I
didn't know your name then, but, well, when I did, I
just—er—didn't tell him that you, my new boss, and—
er—...'

'Your knight in shining armour,' Saville supplied.

'Were one and the same man,' she ended quickly.
'More coffee?'

He laughed. She loved it. Even though she was embarrassed, she loved it when he laughed. 'I've been
called many things in my day—but a knight in shining

armour! Yes, please,' he answered her earlier question, adding quite conversationally, 'You've gone a very pretty pink, Miss Rayner.'

She laughed, not out loud, but inwardly. And later, when they left the restaurant, she was still feeling cheered inside. Saville walked to her car with her and stood for a moment looking down at her.

Then he was taking a step back. 'Goodnight, Edney,' he bade her. And, with a smile there in his voice—she was sure of it—he said, 'Don't worry about a thing—I have every confidence in you.'

Edney felt not only cheered but warmed through and through. 'Goodnight,' she answered quietly, and, forcing herself to get into her car, she said, 'I hope you have a good trip.'

Saville was standing there watching her as she started off, and Edney drove home knowing then, if she hadn't before, that away from the office Saville Craythorne was quite, quite charming.

CHAPTER FOUR

FORGET pleasant, forget charming! Edney went swinging happily, not to say eagerly, into the office on Monday—and was scowled at by Saville Craythorne for her trouble. He had been speaking to Annette, but, with the barest nod in Edney's direction by way of greeting, he turned, strode into his office and firmly closed the door.

'Lovely to have you back, Annette.' She dredged up her manners to warmly welcome the PA back to business—to think she had spent the weekend in looking forward to today! 'How did the holiday go?'

'Splendidly,' Annette beamed, but her mind was obviously already switched to concentrate on work. 'You did very well, I hear.'

Not from Saville Craythorne had she heard it, if Edney was any judge. 'I managed—just. Another week, though, and I'd have been struggling.'

Business got under way and they were, as usual, extremely busy. But not so busy that Edney missed, on the few occasions she caught a glimpse of Saville, that she was most definitely being frowned on. For two pins she would have gone in and asked what she had done wrong. But, no, a girl had her pride. According to Annette, the work she had done had been excellent, her ability to cope in her absence first class. So bubbles to him! Grief, to think she had spent so much as a moment of her time in Bristol at the weekend in thinking, with pleasure, of the wretched man. She wanted her head looking into!

Edney was still feeling decidedly disgruntled on Tuesday—and was still being favoured with indifferent looks from Saville. When, that was, he ever bothered to glance her way.

On Wednesday she started to form the view that, come the end of her three-month trial period—always supposing she lasted that long—she would be on the receiving end of a summons, telling her, You're good, but not good enough.

Which made her think seriously of resigning there and then. But something, she knew not what, seemed to be urging her to stay, to stick it out. Saville was due to go away again soon—Copenhagen, this time. With luck he might never come back.

Around mid-morning Annette glanced at her watch and reached for her bag. Edney knew that Annette's mother was having trouble with her eyes and that Annette was taking her to see a consultant.

'I won't disturb Saville to tell him I'm off. But perhaps you'd go in and mention it in about fifteen minutes? He'll probably be in need of some coffee by then, too.' Annette smiled.

Edney smiled back—as far as she was concerned he could die of thirst before she saw to it that he had a cup of coffee. But, to her way of thinking, the PA had enough on her plate without having to put up with a demurring assistant. 'Leave it with me,' she agreed pleasantly, and spent the next fifteen minutes hoping that her employer might be called upon to go elsewhere and deal with some sudden crisis.

But no such joy. Realising she'd better go and get it over with, Edney left her chair and went to the closed door of the inner sanctum. Tapping lightly on the wood panelling, she went in.

Saville was studying some papers—he didn't look up. 'Annette's gone to keep her appointment,' Edney stated calmly—she had an idea he'd worked that out for himself. No reply. Striving to keep her calm—ignorant pig—

she went over and set to work on pouring him a drink—
he was big enough to pour his own in her opinion. How
do you like your coffee—down the back of your neck?

It was while Edney was nursing such sweet thoughts,
her mind clearly not on what she was doing, that she
was sharply brought to awareness, when she somehow
managed to miss the cup she was holding completely—
and accidentally poured hot coffee over the back of her
left hand.

'Uhh!' she gasped in shock, staring disbelievingly—
replacing the coffee pot on its hot plate with a bang.

'What…?' Saville, alerted by her shocked gasp, spun
round—and took in the situation straight away. 'Go and
put your hand under the cold tap at once,' he ordered.

'The c-carpet!' she spluttered, in shock, not moving.

'*Now!*' he commanded.

'Oh, I'm so sorry. The mess. I'll cl—'

She discovered '*now*' didn't mean tomorrow, it meant
right now. And, to prove it, Saville didn't waste time
arguing. He was out of his chair, and taking a hold of
her by the arm. She obeyed.

He led her quickly to the adjoining washroom and
while he held her hand under the cold running tap he
secured the plug in the basin and filled it with cold water.

At first Edney felt nothing. Then the pain started.
Instinctively she pulled her hand out of the water. Saville
took a hold of her wrist and pushed her hand under
again.

She wanted to tell him that it hurt—excruciatingly—
but thought he probably knew that. She turned her head
away—and discovered it was only a couple of inches
away from his chest. True, the washroom was small, but
she hadn't realised until then just how close they were
standing to each other.

Edney went to pull away. But then, to her amazement,
found that one of Saville's hands had come to the back

of her head and he was urging against him. She didn't know why she suddenly felt tearful, but rather felt it had more to do with the inner sensitivity she had once before seen in Saville than with the pain she was experiencing.

She rested her head against him, was aware that his other arm had come about her and, thus cradled by him, felt at once comforted—*and* tearful.

'You're being very brave,' he encouraged gently.

'Big girls don't cry,' she found out of a shaky nowhere.

'It will ease off soon,' Saville assured her, and Edney felt that she really, really liked him.

For some minutes more they stood like that. Then, as her shock receded, Edney came to, realising she was taking precious minutes out of his working day. 'I think it will be all right now,' she suggested quietly. And realised that Saville must have thought so too when he let go of her and stood back.

But it was he who gently dried her reddened hand and examined it. 'It doesn't look so good,' he commented.

'I think it looks as well as can be expected,' she laughed, not wondering how she could feel mirth after her accident—only knowing that, astonishingly, she was suddenly happy. She glanced up and saw that Saville was staring down at her, his eyes raking her face. 'I'd—er—better—um—get you some more coffee,' she said haltingly, feeling all at once confused.

She hadn't been able to read the expression in his eyes. But, as she turned back into Saville's office, there was no doubting that in his step from the washroom to his office his mood had undergone a very distinct change. For now it was all business—forget your accident—when he clipped shortly, 'I'll make do without.'

'But...' she protested—her protest half at his change of mood; she wanted him back to being gentle and sensitive.

'I haven't time now!' he cut her off sharply, and went to his desk.

Bewildered, she stared after him. 'I'd—er—better clean up the mess; I'm...'

'Leave it!' he ordered—and Edney started to get cross. Too true she'd leave it! She hoped the coffee left a stain in the carpet that would never come out! The phone in her office rang. 'Take it here,' he ordered bossily—but she didn't thank him for his consideration which prevented her doing a sprint back to her own desk.

She then realised that it was a call on the internal phone—which he obviously had already noted. Keeping her expression wooden, Edney picked up the phone and pressed the necessary button to redirect the call. 'Hello?' she said.

'Edney, heartless Edney,' said a voice she would have rather preferred not to know.

'Hello, Felix,' she responded, too late to wish she hadn't mentioned his name. Saville looked none too pleased to hear that his cousin was wasting more of her time.

'I refuse to believe you're busy this Saturday.' Felix was putting on the charm.

'This Saturday,' she repeated. Saville made no attempt to work but just sat there scowling at her. She had trouble in concentrating on what, if anything, she had planned for Saturday.

'I've been invited to a party—I can't go alone.' He made his voice sound desolate.

'Party?' she queried, playing for time. Sometimes she could go for many months and never be invited to a party, now they seemed thicker on the ground than weeds. She thought, though, she'd had enough of parties for the moment.

'Do say you'll come,' Felix urged.

He was still urging when Edney flicked another glance

at her employer. Hostile didn't describe it! Add to that the fact that he was still making no attempt to get on with the work that had been so urgent that he hadn't had time for coffee, but was openly listening to her end of the conversation, and Edney grew more angry—and perhaps a little confused. Quite clearly Saville Craythorne didn't give a button whom she went out with so long as it didn't disrupt his busy office—as this non-business call was doing right now.

'Saturday, you said?' she queried, not pausing to wonder why Saville not caring whom she went out with should upset her, she butted in to what Felix had been saying.

'Say what time I can call for you?' he urged.

Edney took a deep breath. 'You'd better have my address,' she accepted, and as one man sounded positively delighted to her left ear, and the other positively glared at her face, she told Felix where she lived.

Having arranged a time, Edney replaced the phone and was about to return, head high, to her own office, when she somehow felt pulled to glance at her hostile employer again. Hostile—he looked positively murderous!

Startled, she opened her mouth, unsure if she might thank him for the use of his phone. But she didn't get the chance to say anything for the moment, because Saville got in there first.

'I trust your hand will be better by Saturday!' he snarled. Like him? she hated him! Thank him? Like heck!

'I'm sure it won't interfere with anything I want to do!' she returned tartly, and, not trusting herself to say anything else, she got out of there smartly. Go on, fire me—see if I care!

By Saturday she had cooled down enough to wonder what had got into her last Wednesday. She could, she supposed, have still been a little bit in shock after scalding her hand. Thinking about it, although her manner had been a little bit off—well, a lot, if she was honest—what she had retaliated with didn't amount to a dismissable offence, she wouldn't have thought.

Saville, perhaps, thought so too. He hadn't dismissed her anyhow. Maybe he'd made allowances because of her scald. Some people were more prone to shock than others. Maybe he thought she was one of them. Or was he just being fair?

She remembered how gentle and sensitive he had been with her, remembered being cradled against his chest—and, as her heart actually seemed to give a little flip at the memory, Edney decided that she quite liked him again.

She was upstairs when Felix arrived to take her to the party. But Edney did not hurry down to greet him. She heard her father let him in, and, taking up her comb, noticed that her left hand was no longer anywhere near as red as it had been. She knew she had Saville to thank for that. Given that the pain had been quite diabolical at the time, the cold water treatment appeared to have done the trick.

Suddenly Edney became aware that her eyes had gone dreamy. She pulled herself together rapidly, combed her hair, and went down the stairs.

Felix's friends were very nice people, who welcomed them warmly. Then Felix was introducing her to various guests, the party following a long-established format of chatting endlessly, dancing now and again, and of partaking from a quite sumptuous buffet.

For the first two hours of the party Felix was a model escort. Then, unfortunately, starting with the odd scratchy word here, an over-familiar hand on her arm there, his up-to-then perfect manners started to slip. Edney began not to enjoy the party so much as she had.

And, when some late new arrivals suddenly appeared by the drawing room door—a tall, dark-haired man with an elegant, last-word-in-poise blonde on his arm—all at once, as a dreadful sick feeling hit her, Edney started not to enjoy the party at all!

What was *he* doing here? He *knew* she'd be here! He'd no right... Their eyes met. Across that crowded room, as if drawn to each other—utter rot, of course, she realised later—their eyes met.

Very slightly Saville Craythorne inclined his head in her direction. How magnanimous! She wanted to thumb her nose at him—but she had been very well brought up. Ever so slightly she inclined her head in acknowledgement and simultaneously they both turned away.

For the next hour Edney did her best to enjoy the party. She supposed Saville had, with that nod of his head, acknowledged her presence, but all too plainly he wasn't keen on spending any time chatting to her. Keeping his distance wasn't in it! Not that she cared! She'd got nothing she wanted to say to him anyhow.

She had most definitely ceased to enjoy the party. If Felix Stevens put a sneaky arm about her shoulders once more, she was going to have to put him straight.

They were in the drawing room when his arm went about her waist. 'Felix!' she muttered threateningly.

'Let's dance,' he replied, oblivious, it seemed, to the fact she was getting just a tiny bit fed up with him.

About to tell him no, and that she was ready to go home, at that moment she just happened to spot Saville in what looked to her like friendly and intimate conversation with the blonde. What Edney had been about to say went totally from her mind. Somehow, she couldn't bear to stay in the same room.

'Love to,' some actress she hadn't known lived within her answered. That actress even managed to smile up at Felix.

Edney regretted that smile once she and he were in the dance area. Okay, so the music was slow in tempo, but did he have to hold her so tightly? She stuck it for perhaps another thirty seconds, then, when he tightened his grip still further, she gave him a push.

'What?' he enquired, hurt, though not physically.

'You're holding me too closely!' she informed him bluntly. Would the music never end?

'Aw, come on, Edney,' Felix complained and, instead of loosening his hold, he pulled her yet closer still, and proceeded to render her very near speechless when he followed through by bending his head and placing a loose-lipped kiss on her neck.

'Don't *do* that!' she protested when she had got her breath back. Having had just about enough, she was going to give him a more violent push away from her— when someone saved her the bother.

'Mind if I cut in?' enquired a voice she instantly knew. Edney didn't know whether to feel relieved or humiliated when, uncaring if his cousin minded or not, Saville took her from Felix, and the next Edney knew she was gliding around the floor in her employer's arms.

She remembered last Wednesday when he had cradled her to him—but this was nothing like that last time when he had held her. There was nothing gentle or sensitive about him now, nothing but pure out-and-out bossiness when he grated in her ear, 'If you didn't want my cousin's amorous attentions, you shouldn't have encouraged him to begin with!'

Astounded at his attack, Edney pulled back to stare up at him. 'Encouraged?' she questioned on a gasp. Talk about uncompromising—his eyes were pure ice!

'You've been leading him on all evening!' Saville snarled.

'Leading h...' She could not believe she was being so attacked—and in consequence grew rapidly angry.

'You've only been here a little over an hour, so how in blazes would you know?' she challenged furiously.

'It doesn't take a minute to read an enticing glance here, an encouraging smile there!' he clipped aggressively.

'Well, you'd certainly know about that!' she said sarcastically, not doubting that he, with his wealth of experience of women, was a past master at reading all signals! Only he'd got it wrong this time! 'Grief, I can't even smile now without it being misread!' she fumed. And, fed up with the evening—and more than fed up with him, she informed him snappily, 'I've had enough dancing!'

'It isn't over yet! I'll tell you when!' he had the nerve to inform her curtly.

Get him! 'You may be my boss Monday to Friday!' she hissed. 'But we're not in the office now!'

'You should read the small print!' he shot back at her before she could blink.

'Small print?' she echoed witlessly.

'It may not be written—yet—but I thought you understood that you were employed to be available at all reasonable times.'

She stared at him. Was he saying that she was on company business now? The music stopped. She was glad of it—she still hadn't made up her mind. 'Had that been a pleasure, I'd have said thank you,' she offered tartly, as Saville's hands fell to his sides—and with that she walked smartly away from him. He hadn't thanked her either, so she reckoned the feeling was mutual.

She saw Felix looking to head her off. She was in no mood to talk to him just then, and pointed to indicate she was going to the upstairs cloakroom. Men!

Slowly, and it took some minutes, Edney simmered down. As kind as their hosts were, she had definitely had enough of the party. She left the makeshift cloak-room and went to find Felix.

'Would you mind very much if we leave now?' She politely phrased her determination to go within the next five minutes.

Felix positively beamed. 'Love to!' he answered enthusiastically, and Edney began to have serious doubts about allowing him to drive her home. Although she did not seem to have much of an alternative—or so she thought.

Having said goodbye to their hosts, they were seated in Felix's car, which, for the past five minutes, he had tried, without success, to start. He turned to her. 'Problem?' she enquired nicely.

'It won't start!' He stated the obvious.

'Perhaps the rain's got onto the plugs.' She aired her knowledge.

'Do you think so?' he questioned, plainly no mechanic. It had rained, yes, but only lightly, and nothing at all like the deluge that had incapacitated her vehicle that time.

'Er—do you think you should get out and take a look?' she suggested tentatively—it wasn't her idea of fun to sit in his car all night.

'I could—but my cluelessness about a car's innards is the family joke,' he replied, and, smiling, he turned to her—lechery in his every line as he leaned forward and opined, 'We could start a party of our own right here, little Edney.'

She was grateful for small mercies and reckoned she was lucky that they were parked where they were, and not in some isolated spot, only to find that the car wouldn't start.

'At the risk of...' She was just about to get started on sorting him out, when someone came and tapped on the driver's window.

Felix, recognising it was Saville, as did Edney, got out from the car. 'You're not getting much response, from what I heard,' she heard Saville comment. He must be meaning the car; he couldn't have heard her—or her tone. 'Having trouble?' Saville asked.

'Edney thinks the rain may have got onto the plugs,' she heard Felix reply—and wanted to crawl into a hole with embarrassment.

She was still feeling mortified when Saville answered, 'Does she now?' A pause and then, decisive as always, he continued, 'If that's the case it's unlikely they'll dry out before morning—I suppose I'd better do the cousinly thing and give you a lift.'

She'd walk! On broken glass if she had to—but Felix was already thanking Saville and ducking back inside the car to tell her what was happening. Edney put it down to her discomfiture at having her lack of mechanical knowledge publicly aired—and the certainty that Saville knew full well it would take a lot more than a bit of drizzle to put a car of this quality out of action— that she protested not a peep, but left Felix's vehicle and went down the drive some way with him and his cousin, to where Saville had parked his car.

Saville unlocked his car, and while Felix held open the rear passenger door for her Saville held open the front passenger door, remarking smoothly, to her great amazement, 'You'd better sit up front with me, Edney. Then you can direct me to where you live.'

He'd forgotten! She didn't believe it! Twice he'd driven to her home and hadn't needed the merest direction the second time! He gave a small impatient sound because she wasn't galloping to obey his summons, and, bearing in mind he was doing both her and Felix a favour in leaving the party and giving them a lift, she got in, more meekly than she would have liked.

What he had been doing out on the drive in the first

place, when the blonde he'd arrived with was nowhere around, was a mystery. Perhaps he'd needed a little air... 'Won't your friend mind—er—waiting?' she began before she could think.

The self-assured look he gave her—as if he'd be amazed if there was a woman breathing who wouldn't mind waiting for him—said it all. Smug pig! Edney decided that she was not going to volunteer another word, and left what conversation there was to him and his cousin, who was leaning forward from the rear passenger seat.

Though she found it impossible to refrain from mentioning, as a junction in the road came nearer and nearer—and Saville already started to slow down—sweetly but entirely unnecessarily, 'We take a left turn here.'

When they arrived outside her home both men got out of the car, though she supposed that Saville must be the fitter of the two, since he was at the passenger door first. 'Do you have your key?' he enquired, quite curtly she thought, as he waited for her to vacate his car.

She retrieved the key from her purse to show him. He took it from her and, before she could so much as blink, he had gone to the front door of her rambling house. Inserting the key in the lock, he opened the door for her.

So, okay, he had a blonde to get back to, but really! 'Goodnight,' she said crisply, seeing Felix approaching, but in no mood for another kiss on her neck, particularly with Saville this close. 'Goodnight, Felix,' she bade him hurriedly, adding a pretty, 'Thank you for the party,' before bolting indoors.

Wretch! Monster! Diabolical swine! It was not Felix, however, who was the object of such affections, but his overbearing, lordly, must-get-back-to-the-blonde cousin. She was never, ever, going to another party again!

Well, she qualified, as she climbed into bed, she *might* go to another party, but if she did—and if *he* was there—then she was going to leave straight away!

CHAPTER FIVE

MONDAY arrived and Edney was still trying to put the events of Saturday evening out of her head. Though why it should in any way bother her that Saville Craythorne was such a bossy, arrogant swine, she didn't know. She'd realised that before the party, for goodness' sake!

And what had he meant by 'yet'? 'It may not be written—yet,' he'd said, when he'd mentioned she was employed to be available at all reasonable times. Had he been suggesting that she would have it written into her contract, when she gained a permanent job in his office? That was if she completed her three-month trial period successfully.

Or, had he meant exactly the opposite? That 'yet' niggled away at her. Had Saville merely been warning her that from now on, if she was to have any chance of making it, she should be on her best behaviour?

But, in fairness, he must see that okay, she wasn't up to Annette's standard yet—but she had coped quite well in Annette's absence; well, she had thought she had.

Edney felt her heartbeat hurry at the thought of permanently working in the next-door office to Saville. Bossy, arrogant swine he might be, but working for and with him was stimulating, exciting—even when working under pressure.

And, though she had been working under pressure while Annette was away, she had coped, and would cope. So Saville must mean, despite the curt way he had parted from her on Saturday, that she might be able to stay.

Having reached the most hopeful conclusion, there

was a spring in Edney's step when she went breezing into her office. Both Saville and Annette were in his office she saw at once through the open door, and a bright 'Good morning!' escaped her before she could stop it.

Saville stared at her, his unsmiling countenance telling her that he was totally unimpressed by her chic skirt, top and generally immaculate appearance.

'Close the door on your way out,' he instructed Annette, his eyes still on Edney.

She looked away; quite clearly, 'Close the door' meant he'd seen all of her that he wanted to. The door closed. She looked at Annette, who smiled and greeted her, 'Good morning, Edney. Pleasant weekend?'

'Lovely. How about you?'

They discussed the merits of gardening for a few moments, then Annette remarked apologetically, 'I'm afraid we're in for one of those weeks. Things are happening at our Copenhagen branch, and, unless they can be sorted by Friday, there'll be nothing for it but for Saville to fly over.'

'As bad as that?' Edney queried, aware that Saville already had a full diary this week.

'I'm afraid so—though it's nothing he can't handle. I'm on standby to go with him,' she added.

Edney had been aware from snippets of conversation here and there that Annette occasionally travelled with Saville when he required an assistant on his business trips. By the sound of it—and despite his 'yet'—Edney was well enough trusted to take charge of the office, should Annette have to go on Friday.

Feeling sure that must augur well for the time when her trial period came to an end, Edney worked with a will, and it was half past eleven before she knew it. Saville was waiting for the paperwork she was completing. She left her desk and discovered, quite ridiculously, that she was inwardly trembling at the thought of going in to see him.

Just how ridiculous was borne out by the fact that he didn't so much as glance at her as she went in. She laid the papers on his desk to the side of him. He looked up then.

He seemed tired, she thought, and then she felt all soft inside about him. 'Would you like some coffee?' she asked gently, saw his gaze go from her eyes to the curve of her mouth, then back again—and sorely wished that she had saved her breath.

For he rapped abrasively, 'I'll pour my own!'

'You've got a stain on your carpet!' she snapped—and did a rapid about-turn.

Oh, what was the matter with her? She hoped he knew she was referring to the fact that although a cleaner had made heroic attempts to remove the coffee marks, the results of her accident last week were still faintly visible to someone who knew where to look.

Miserable toad! He'd gone back to that party on Saturday night to collect the blonde—no wonder he was looking tired! Edney had witnessed Saville effortlessly turn over tremendous mountains of work—he thrived on it—so she doubted that pressure of business exhausted him! Pour him a cup of coffee! Like heck! He could be as parched as the Sahara before she'd make another offer to pour him a cup!

Edney had simmered down by the next day, and was on a much more even keel by Wednesday. She stopped questioning what was the matter with her because she had imagined that she had been inwardly trembling when she had gone in to see Saville. It was just the waiting to see if she would be taken on by him as a staff member that was getting to her, that was all. Trembling? Ridiculous!

Ridiculous or not, Edney became aware that, whatever

the reason, Saville Craythorne's very presence in the same room seemed to have a very unsettling effect on her. For it was on Thursday morning, when Saville came in to query something with Annette—he hadn't so much as flicked the briefest of glances Edney's way and she was keen to show that she hadn't noticed him either—that, in closing one of her desk drawers, she somehow, her mind totally elsewhere, managed to shut the drawer most painfully on her thumb.

She would have sworn that she made no cry as she instinctively jerked her thumb clear and, keeping her face impassive—she'd scream later—she carried on working, so no one would be aware that anything had happened.

But, wouldn't you know it, when, early that afternoon, she had to go into the room next-door for some papers, it was to discover that someone was aware of practically everything that went on in the outer office.

Saville didn't look up but carried on with what he was doing, his interest solely on the job in hand. Edney spotted what she had come in for and she leaned over to pick up the papers. Though his attention apparently was still on what he was doing, she distinctly heard him enquire, 'How's the finger?'

Startled, she stared at him—he had seemed oblivious to her. 'Thumb!' she corrected, and, feeling a most idiotic desire to break out into a grin, she quickly got out of there.

She knew as she drove to the office on Friday that she would be in charge of it that afternoon. Matters had not been satisfactorily resolved in Copenhagen and Saville, after a ten o'clock conference, was going straight on to the airport. The short conference was scheduled to take two hours, but, just in case it ran over, Annette, who would be working the whole weekend in

Copenhagen with Saville, had decided to drive herself to the airport independently.

'Good morning, Edney,' Annette greeted her when she went in.

Edney returned her greeting with a smile—and, observing at the same time that the door to Saville's office was closed, experienced totally unexpectedly a most dejected feeling that, if he had nothing he wanted to communicate with Annette before he went, it would be Monday—three whole days—before she saw him again.

Edney immediately scoffed at such a notion. Goodness—why should she feel in any way dejected? He'd been a brute all week! So, okay, he had—without so much as trying—managed to make her want to grin yesterday, but otherwise he'd been like a bear with a sore head.

To prove what a nonsense any such notion was, when Annette left her desk and headed in the direction of Saville's office, Edney—so she should not see him through the open door—deliberately opted to find something she needed from one of the cabinets on the other side of the room. She also managed to be there when Annette came out again.

Annette, no doubt, had discussed all that needed to be discussed with Saville before she saw him again at the airport. Oddly, Edney didn't feel any better for having made sure that she would not see her employer again before Monday.

Though, in actual fact, when she had thought he would leave his office for the ten o'clock conference by the outer door, it was actually via their door that he went.

At five minutes to ten, Saville's office door opened and, briefcase in hand, he strode through. Stupidly, Edney's heart lurched. It was totally absurd, she decided—Saville, tall, handsome and quite superb in his faultlessly tailored suit, wasn't even looking at her but addressed some remark to Annette.

He did have something to say to her, though, as he headed for the door. 'You've enough to do to keep you out of mischief?' he enquired.

Was he being funny? She seldom seemed to stop! Edney stared up at him; his expression was stern—he *wasn't* being funny. She resisted the impulse to tell him she had thought about swinging from the chandelier in her spare time, and managed to eye him steadily as she replied, 'I save getting into mischief for the weekends.'

'I noticed!' he gritted—and she thought she experienced a feeling of dejection again that she wouldn't see him. She must be going soft in the head!

He hadn't been gone ten seconds, however, when his cousin was on the phone, asking her to go out with him again. She remembered his damp kiss on her neck, and the look in his eyes that spoke of ideas in his head which had never been in hers.

'Sorry, Felix, I'm going away this weekend.' No need for him to know she was going to Bristol tomorrow, not tonight. 'Did you get your car repaired, by the way?'

'You must have been right about the rain getting in. It started first time when Saville dropped me over to pick it up on Sunday. You're sure you're going away? You're not…?'

'I'm sure,' she replied, and hinted, 'I'm extremely busy, Felix.'

Eventually she managed to say goodbye to him—then answered another personal call, though this time not for herself but for Annette, who took it from her. Before Edney could take up her work again, she became aware from listening to Annette's side of the conversation that something was very wrong.

Confirmation of this lay in the fact that, as Annette terminated her call, Edney could see for herself the PA's sudden pallor and worried look. 'What's wrong?' she asked, wanting to help when Annette's front, normally calm and able to cope with anything, started to slip.

'My mother...' Annette began in fractured tones. 'That was her friend—the woman who was going to stay with her while I was away. Mother's had a fall, a serious one. They're waiting for the ambulance.'

'You must go,' Edney urged, work of secondary importance.

'Yes, I must,' Annette agreed, and was already reaching for her bag when she seemed to surface a little from her first immediate shock to realise she was in an office environment and that there were other matters to consider.

'Would you like me to drive you?' Edney queried. 'You don't...'

'You've got your car here?'

It was an odd question, considering she had driven herself in every day, barring that one day her father had given her a lift. But shock did funny things to people. 'It's in the car park.'

'Good,' Annette replied, and, clearly getting her head together, checked her watch and began instantly working out probables and possibles—while at the same time wanting to be out of there fast. 'My mother's going to need X-rays—I'm likely to be at the hospital for hours.' She let Edney into some of her thoughts, and then promptly frightened the daylights out of her by declaring positively, 'You'll have to go to Copenhagen for me.'

Edney stared at her in disbelief. *'Me!'* she exclaimed, startled—and had further proof, if proof were needed, of what a very brilliant PA Annette Lewis was.

In minutes, while Edney was desperately wanting to protest that she couldn't go—and did Saville need an assistant with him anyway?—Annette was reeling off scores of things Edney should do, take, note—and she shouldn't forget the office laptop. While Edney was still trying to get to grips with the astonishing fact that though she had been thinking she wouldn't see Saville again until Monday, it now looked as if she had been steam-rollered into spending the entire weekend with him—unless she could find a jolly good reason not to go—Annette was explaining where at the airport—since apparently they were flying in a private jet—Saville would expect to see his assistant.

While taking all this on board—and wondering if the fact that her mother expected at least ten days' notice if she planned to miss her fortnightly visit to Bristol would be good excuse enough for her not to go mdney also recalled Saville's diktat of last Saturday, when he'd instructed that she was employed to be available at all reasonable times.

Oh, help! 'Er—you don't think Pippa would be better equipped to go?' she questioned tentatively, fully in agreement that, under the circumstances, Annette's place was at the hospital with her mother, not in Denmark.

'Pippa? No—no.' Annette shook her head. 'You've been working on the Copenhagen stuff on and off all week. It would take much too long to brief her. Besides, you're more than up to it,' she added encouragingly.

Edney started to feel mean. 'Of course,' she smiled, putting her nerves aside. 'Go to your mother, Annette. I'll cope, I promise.' Wishing she felt as confident as she'd forced herself to sound, Edney had only one more question before—as Annette had instructed—she raced home to pack a bag and pick up her passport. 'Shall I ring through to the conference room to let Saville know what's happening?'

'Heavens, no! Apart from the fact that there deliberately isn't a phone in there, Saville would have your hide if you interrupted this meeting for anything short of an earthquake.' Annette was on her way through the door when she called back, 'You can fill him in when you see him at the airport.'

'Hope things will be all right with your mother,' Edney said gently. She had very little time after that to think of Mrs Lewis, Annette, or anything other than the job in hand.

She was racing home to pack her bag, tell her father—and phone her mother—when, more fearsomely than that, she realised that there was someone else she was going to have to tell she was going to go to Copenhagen. She was going to have to tell Saville Craythorne that she was accompanying him on the Denmark trip!

She remembered his stern I-hate-Edney-Rayner expression of a few hours earlier. Remembered his short way with her all this week. Oh, brother, he was just going to love turning up at the airport and finding her there!

'You realise I shall have to eat out tonight,' was her father's comment when she told him she was dashing off the moment she had her things together. Though she could tell he looked tickled pink that his little girl was so well thought of at I. L. Engineering that she was flying off with the chairman, no less—she wished she felt the same!

'You could try cooking for yourself,' she suggested.

'Perish that thought,' he answered glumly, but cheered up as he asked, 'Have you told your mother yet?'

'Not yet,' Edney replied.

'Would you like me to?' he offered gleefully.

'No, I wouldn't!' she returned, a shade edgily, it had to be admitted.

Then she found, not for the first time, what a lovely parent she had. Because straight away he read her edginess and was there for her, his pride in her not one tiny bit dented as he stated seriously, 'You know, sweetheart, you don't have to go if you don't want to.'

Feeling instantly and thoroughly ashamed of herself, Edney took a moment to think about it and wrestle with her nerves. Then she smiled. 'You know, Dad, I rather think I want to go.'

Edney was having gigantic second thoughts about that as she, miraculously, after her mad rush-around, was the first at the airport. She had an idea that Saville would go ape when she acquainted him with the fact that she would be assisting him this trip. Against that, though—and she was desperately searching for a counter-argument—I. L. Engineering was a highly professional outfit. There was a job to be done—surely personalities, and the fact that Saville had seemed to be down on her this week, didn't come into it.

It bothered her more than she felt it should that Saville had been hard put to spare her a word all week, so Edney tried to pin her thoughts on other matters. Her mother, to put it mildly, had not been best pleased that her daughter wouldn't be driving down to Bristol to see her tomorrow. Statements, such as, 'Inconsiderate! For goodness' sake, they don't *own* you! Resign—find yourself another job,' had all flown heatedly over the telephone wires. The trouble was, Edney didn't want another job—she wanted this one.

Which just shows how crazy I must be, she mused a minute and a half later when her employer strode into view. He spotted her immediately, and the weekend bag down by her feet, plus office laptop—with no sign of his PA.

Saville came over and halted close enough for Edney to see into his eyes. And it was then, for all it was high summer, that she wished she was wearing her winter coat—Arctic didn't cover it!

'Annette's m-mother—she had an accident!' she blurted out before he could demand what in thunder she was doing there. 'Annette can't come. I—she sent me instead.'

A grunt was all she received for her trouble, and a muttered, 'That's all I need!' He turned from her. She picked up her belongings. He went striding away—she chased after him. Thanks, Edney! Thanks for dropping everything and rushing here to assist me, Edney! Thanks for upsetting your mother, Edney! I'm truly, truly grateful, Edney! Kiss my feet, Edney! She wanted to use her feet—to crack his shin! He needed her more than she needed him—remember that, Edney!

He halted and she nearly cannoned into him. He froze her with a look—and her overstretched nerves of the past few hours snapped and got the better of her. 'If you'd rather I wasn't here, I can just as soon go back to the office!' she flared. Oh, great—a fine way to keep the job she was so anxious to hang on to!

She opened her mouth again—then found that it wasn't in her to apologise. Then she discovered that he wasn't dismissing her on the spot for her attitude, but that she still had a job, when he ordered succinctly, 'Shut up! Have you checked you've got everything with you that you'll need?'

Far be it from her to say another word. She nodded. In actual fact, save for filling him in on the little she knew about the fall which Annette's mother had suffered, not very much in the way of conversation passed between Edney and her employer on the flight to Denmark.

They were met at Copenhagen's airport and driven to their hotel. Saville, she discovered, had a suite, and she had a room on the same floor near at hand. Close enough, she assumed sourly, to ensure she and her laptop would arrive in mere seconds should he require some urgent input—regardless of the hour. They were there to work!

And work they did. Barely had they dropped off their bags at the hotel than they were off to a late afternoon meeting. It was, she observed, a veritable hornets' nest of argument and counter-argument. She was amazed that the nine people present—six men, three women—all spoke fluent English and were able to put their viewpoints concisely and clearly in a language that was not their first.

Edney took pages of notes and had to admit to feeling no end of pride at the way Saville listened attentively, deliberated briefly, then politely issued decisions with a tact and charm that was little short of stunning. At sticking points he pleasantly decreed they couldn't do any better than to sleep on them, and left those matters in abeyance until the following morning.

The fact that they would all be working on Saturday seemed incidental. The meeting broke up and Edney and Saville were first to leave. They were going down in the lift when she glanced at her watch. No wonder Saville had ended discussions for the day. It was ten past eight!

She looked up in astonishment—and saw that Saville had been watching her. 'What happened to ten past six and ten past seven?' she exclaimed.

'I hardly noticed either,' he answered, his eyes gentle on her. It was one of those very rare moments where they seemed to be as one. Edney felt all soft inside—she wouldn't mind the least little bit working until ten past midnight. The moment did not last. Saville's eyes seemed to have iced over when he followed up with, 'If you get all that typed into your laptop tonight we can start afresh tomorrow.'

'Perhaps I could have a sandwich in between paragraphs,' she answered snappily—no need to tell him that she couldn't remember having had time for lunch.

He didn't deign to answer, and Edney realised that if she was to stand a dog's chance of keeping this job, which she coveted so much, she was going to seriously have to guard her tongue. She didn't know what it was about him—she was sure she never used to be so snappy—but he seemed to have an unerring knack of making her rear up!

They arrived back at their hotel without another word passing between them. But, since he was her boss, once the lift had deposited them at their floor, Edney made an effort. 'I'll see that everything is put on disk tonight,' she began. Coming to his suite first, he halted, and she paused before going along to her own room.

'You're bound to have some queries,' he clipped. 'You'd better work in here.'

He was right; she knew he was. If she worked in his sitting room it would save her ringing him every so often—by the sound of it, he was staying in.

'Very well,' she said primly, and waited for him to unlock the door to his suite.

'Freshen up first,' he instructed, and abruptly she wheeled away.

Thanks! If that was his way of saying that she looked a wreck, she didn't need it. In her room, she not only freshened up but changed into some tailored trousers and a white overshirt. So—she was still working, but to blazes with it, she'd been wearing what she called 'business clothes' all day. However, she was here to work, so after flicking a comb through her long red tresses, with laptop in hand, Edney left her room.

Surprise number one came when Saville opened the door to her knock: he had changed from his business suit too, and was now clad in casual trousers and a shirt. She smiled at him—how could she not? Clearly he had felt as weary of his business clothes as she. Perhaps it was even from thoughtfulness on his part that he had sent her to freshen up.

'Come in,' he invited, his eyes on her smiling countenance—for once there was no sign of ice in his eyes.

'Hope I haven't kept you waiting,' she commented,
suddenly shaky.

He didn't answer, but ushered her into a kind of sit-
ting-room-cum-dining-room, where surprise number two
awaited. Room service had been and gone—and had left
behind a couple of plates of sandwiches and some coffee.

She turned. 'You...'

'Sandwiches, as requested,' Saville cut in smoothly—
and she just had to grin. Apparently she was forgiven
for her snappy comment about 'a sandwich between paragraphs'.

'You intended to order something to eat all along,
didn't you?' she questioned.

'Have to fuel you if I want any work out of you,' he
answered. Edney didn't take umbrage, but accepted then
that he had the power to mix up her head more than
anyone she knew, and realised also that he must be starving as well. 'Tuck in,' he invited.

'I am mildly ravenous,' she confessed prettily, and—
wonder of wonders—actually saw his mouth pick up at
the corners—as if he found her a tinge amusing.

Inside fifteen minutes, however, the sandwiches were
eaten, the coffee finished, and they were hard at it, dealing with more serious matters. For the next hour and a
half Edney slaved at the dining table while Saville
worked with pen and paper from the sofa. He was right,
of course, she did have to consult him from time to time
with some query or other. But she was not sorry when
at ten o'clock, more coffee arrived and Saville decreed
she should have a ten-minute break.

He poured her a cup of coffee; she wanted to smile
again, strangely in no way offended that he wasn't trusting her to pour. 'Thank you,' she murmured politely

when, towering over her, he came and placed a cup and saucer on the table.

'It's I who should thank you,' he replied evenly.

Edney heard him return to the sofa and turned round on her seat. 'You should?' she questioned, not with him.

'For dropping everything—your weekend plans—at a moment's notice to stand in for Annette.'

Grief—they were coming on! He was actually thanking her! 'No problem,' she commented.

'You didn't have plans for the weekend?'

She stared at him—he truly did seem interested. 'I—um—did actually,' she corrected, and saw his expression go from faintly affable to faintly hostile. Now what had she said?

'I trust he was understanding?'

As if *he* cared! Not that she was likely to explain that it wasn't a he, but that the most exciting thing she had been planning to do that weekend was to go shopping with her mother. 'There'll be other weekends,' she said daintily, and guessed her ten-minute break was over after five minutes when to show just how interested he was, Saville finished his coffee and picked up his pen.

One of these days she'd find out just how his mind worked—he was never the same two minutes together! Edney resumed work, wondering if she would be allowed to work in his office at I. L. Engineering long enough to find out more about him.

Perhaps having to cope with his moods was some sort of test? She rejected the notion. What she saw was what she got—Saville didn't have time to mess about. And certainly assistant PA's were two a penny from where he was viewing it, so why would he bother?

Three quarters of an hour later and she was starting to wilt. She wanted her bed. It had been a long day— and yet, most unfathomably, there seemed a reluctant part of her that didn't want to go to her room. It was almost as if she wanted to stay exactly where she was. She *must* be tired! She referred to her notebook but the paper in it, like many of the same sort, had a sharp edge.

'Oh!'' she exclaimed involuntarily.

'What's wrong?'

From nowhere Saville was suddenly there. She felt a fool. 'Nothing. I just—nicked my finger,' she muttered—and felt a charge go through her like a shot of electricity when, totally unexpectedly, he caught a hold of her right hand and raised it for inspection.

'I don't think it will need a stitch,' he offered seriously after examining the merest trace of blood that had appeared from the tiniest scratch.

He was teasing! Incredibly, Edney realised he was teasing her! 'You—er—don't think I should seek a second opinion?' she questioned solemnly, weariness falling from her in an instant.

'Are you casting aspersions, young woman?' he growled. Edney knew then that she really, really liked him. She wasn't sure as she looked up into his dark eyes that there wasn't a glimmer of laughter in them. Was he a master at disguising his emotions?

'Would I dare?' she replied, and was fully aware that he still had a hold of her hand, though she was less aware that her thinking was definitely going haywire— like her co-ordination! 'I never used to be accident-prone,' she felt it necessary to defend herself; something just seemed to happen to her concentration when Saville was anywhere around. 'M-may I have my hand back, please?' she just had to request—her brain didn't seem to be working properly while his skin touched her skin!

In an instant he had let go of her hand—and some sense of normality returned to Edney. She still stared up at him, though, and owned to feeling quite witless when, staring back down at her, Saville remarked, 'You're all eyes, young lady.' While she seemed too mesmerised to turn back to her work, he continued, 'I think you'd better get off to bed.'

'I'm not a nine-year-old!' spurted from her before she could stop it.

'I never for a moment believed that you were,' he shot back. Was that a compliment? She wasn't sure. 'But what you are is tired.'

'But—' she started to protest. 'I haven't finished yet.'

'I can finish off here.'

'You type?' She wanted to laugh at the absurd suggestion, but didn't.

'What I meant was that I'll finish off what I need to do, and…' a wicked light entered his eyes '…you can finish what you need to do in the morning.' Before she could remind him that they had a meeting at ten a.m. sharp—and to prove he didn't need reminding of the least little thing—he said, 'We don't have to be there until ten—you'll have plenty of time.'

'Perhaps you'll ask the cook to make me a bacon roll to eat on the way!'

She laughed once she got to her room. He was a swine. A loveable swine. Loveable! Good grief! Realising that she must be more tired than she knew, Edney had a quick shower and went to bed.

But she didn't get to sleep straight away. Somehow she began to see that for all Saville still maintained a hard edge with her for the most part, there was a part of him coming through that was making him more approachable than he had been.

And, on the word 'approachable', she mused that she had worked in his office for eight weeks now. Surely it wasn't too soon to approach Saville and ask how her three-month trial period was going? And she fell asleep.

Edney was in a deep and dreamless sleep when the ringing of the telephone brought her up from the depths. 'Hello?' she answered groggily. It was the hotel recep-

tion with her morning alarm call. 'Thank you,' she answered automatically, and struggled into a sitting posi-
tion.

Shaking off remnants of sleep, she glanced at her
travel alarm clock—and came fully awake. It was five
to six! She had no memory whatsoever of ordering a
wake-up call! Why would she, when she had set her
alarm to go off at a quarter to seven?

Edney was suddenly wide awake. The rat! Saville
Craythorne must have ordered that call! Right! One up,
everybody up! Edney dived for the bathroom, took the
quickest shower on record, threw on her underclothes,
applied a light make-up. Then, with expertise, she
flipped her long red hair into a neat chignon and donned
a smart suit of deep blue.

Slipping on her shoes as she went, Edney grabbed up
her bag on the way and, at just gone half-past-six, she
rapped lightly on the door of Saville's rooms. She expected to have to wait. Expected to have to knock again,
more loudly. Expected that, when Saville did eventually
open his door, he would be bleary-eyed and unshaven.

Not so! The door opened almost immediately and,
shaved, groomed and immaculately suited, Saville
looked back at her. Her heart thundered crazily and she
found she was in desperate need of something to say.

'I hope I didn't keep you waiting,' she huskily found
from somewhere.

He smiled; he actually smiled. She felt warmed
through and through. 'You're still half asleep,' he accused softly.

Edney guessed she had her husky voice to thank for
that remark. 'Lies, all lies,' she grinned and, her heart
well and truly misbehaving, she stepped past him into
the suite. What the Dickens was the matter with her?

She heard Saville close the door and he followed her
into the sitting room. Two large trays of breakfast had

already arrived, she noted. 'I hope the wake-up call wasn't too early,' Saville remarked as she turned to face him.

He cared! That was a first! 'Oh, no,' she answered as airily as she was capable of being, given that just looking at him seemed to be having some peculiar effect on her. 'I'd already set my travel alarm, though,' she added lightly. No need for him to know the time she had set it for.

Saville seemed in good humour, but, from experience, Edney knew better than to count on that good humour lasting too long. But he seemed content to chat conversationally as they breakfasted on ham, cheese and coffee. And it was she who tidied up her tray and, ready to begin work, resumed from where she had left off the evening before.

Her capricious heartbeats had settled themselves down by the time her work was completed and they were ready to leave the hotel to go to the ten o'clock meeting. Yet she had to own to feeling a flutter of something inside her—pride, she rather thought—when she walked at his side through the lobby of the hotel and out to their waiting car and driver.

The meeting continued on from yesterday. They had a short break for lunch some time after one, and again resumed. Edney's pride, pride in her employer and the deft way he had handled negotiations, knew no bounds.

It was nearing six by the time all matters were satisfactorily resolved. Then it was handshakes and smiles all around as they left the meeting. She was thrilled to have been part of it—albeit that her part was never likely to shatter empires.

'We've finished early, haven't we?' she asked as their car drove them back to their hotel.

'You're desperate to get home?' Saville asked sharply, before she could draw another breath.

'With such splendid and charming company I should want to stay!' she exploded before she could think. He could be charming to everyone else, but, apparently, not to her!

Nevertheless she almost apologised straight away—that was one fine way to keep her job! But she was glad she hadn't managed to find the words to say she was sorry when, to her amazement, Saville apologised instead.

'Forgive me, Edney. I'm calling a meeting for eleven on Monday—my mind was on the work we still have to do before then.'

'Would I dare let you down?' she replied, and, feeling choked suddenly, she turned her head to look out of the side window. Think of something funny, do! She felt weepy all at once, and would just about have died if so much as one single solitary tear had escaped. For goodness' sake, what *was* the matter with her? She couldn't ever remember being this emotional before!

'If we can get everything done tonight,' Saville continued, 'and it seems more efficient to complete the work here rather than go home now and work from the office tomorrow—we can fly back in the morning.'

'That's fine by me,' she agreed quietly. It had crossed her mind, given she accepted she was not there on holiday, that she might get to take a look round the Tivoli gardens while she was in Copenhagen, and see the statue of Hans Christian Andersen's fairy tale Little Mermaid—that was a must too. But forget that—some other time.

On reaching their hotel, and getting out of the lift at their floor, Edney, while acknowledging that she felt a mixture of edginess and emotion, had no intention of giving Saville the chance to tell her, as he had yesterday to 'freshen up first'.

'Fifteen minutes!' she informed him as they reached

his door, and, not waiting for his answer, she carried on walking until she reached her own room.

She couldn't resist a glance back, though, as she unlocked her door—Saville hadn't entered his suite as she had fully expected, but was standing there watching her. Oh, Lord, she felt all of a tremble inside. The door was open, so quickly she put herself on the other side of it, leaning against it, knowing while at the same time denying that she felt attracted to her employer. Oh, for goodness' sake, get yourself together!

Edney stretched that fifteen minutes to twenty. She needed to. At the end of those twenty minutes, however, she reckoned she had herself more in hand. She had taken another quick shower, applied fresh powder and lipstick and dressed in yesterday's trousers and a fresh shirt; with her rich red hair loose about her shoulders, she felt more in control than she had.

She left her room, reminding herself that personalities didn't come into it. She was there to work, and work she would. Saville answered her knock, and when she had been about to apologise for taking the extra five minutes, she changed her mind. From the look of his damp hair, he had showered too.

'Eager!' he commented when, entering the sitting room she walked straight to the work-table. 'Come and have a cup of tea first.'

Something inside her seemed to thaw. 'I'd love one,' she smiled, and, seeing a tray of tea set on a low table, she went over and poured a couple of cups. She handed Saville one, but experienced such a feeling of restlessness that she took her own tea over to the window and, barely taking in the scene below, stood looking out. Then, as she sipped her tea, that edgey feeling returned. She emptied her cup and commented, 'The sooner I start, the sooner I finish,' and got down to clearing the day's work.

She did not work alone. Saville was busy too, except for when she turned round with a query, or when he wanted to give her some instruction, his pen racing over the pad in his hand. Though he wasn't so busy that he forgot to 'fuel' her. Dinner, which he must have ordered previously, arrived around eight.

She was glad of the break, and slipped into his bathroom to wash her hands. He seemed to instinctively know that she wanted something only light—she just wouldn't be able to work on an over-full stomach, though she was more than ready for the omelette and salad.

'Wine?' Saville enquired, his hand going to the bottle he had ordered.

She shook her head. 'Better not.' She grinned. 'That is unless you want me falling asleep over a hot laptop.'

Saville's eyes flicked to her sweetly curving mouth. 'You're tired—I'm overworking you!' he said regretfully, his glance moving back to her eyes.

'Not at all!' she denied stoutly, ready to work on till dawn if she had to.

'Would you prefer to leave all this until the morning? Until you've had a night's rest?'

Edney was startled that he was being so considerate. But he had been working too, and she gathered he wanted all this out of the way so that he could have tomorrow afternoon off, ready to start afresh on Monday.

'I'd rather get on,' she decided firmly. 'As you said, if we get it all completed tonight, then we can go home in the morning.'

'You've a date tomorrow afternoon?' he questioned, somewhat abrasively, she felt, given that up until then he had seemed considerate to the point of being affable.

'Not particularly,' she answered airily, not averse to giving him the impression that should she require a date it merely required the lifting of the telephone to have half a dozen come running. Though…

Suddenly something occurred to her. Was Saville being grouchy about boyfriends—dates—because he wanted continuity in his office? Because there was no place in his office for assistant PAs who were likely to leave to get married, to start a family, to…

Did he, in fact, want her as dedicated to her job as Annette was to hers? She thought of that 'It may not be written—yet' in relation to her employment, and it seemed an ideal moment to ask—her reliability was without question, she would have thought, or she wouldn't be there now—that very important question of how her trial period was going.

'Er…' Where to start? She had his attention. 'May I ask—er…?'

'Ye-es?' he encouraged, amusement suddenly seeming to light his eyes.

'I—um—wondered—' She broke off. Perhaps Annette was the person she should ask. Edney felt she would be able to take it better from Annette. She'd just about disintegrate if—when he'd stopped laughing—Saville wiped his eyes and answered, Not a prayer.

'When did you ever weigh your words?' Saville questioned good-humouredly when she hesitated still. She supposed he was right.

'I…' she tried again.

Then she saw that Saville was all at once looking serious, though his tone was mild when he suggested, 'This must be pretty heavy stuff, Edney.'

'Not really,' she managed. 'I just sort of wondered if—if this was a good time to ask—how my—um—trial period is going?' There, it was out—not that she felt any better for it; she was strangely hot and bothered as she waited for his answer.

Oddly, however, when she had personally witnessed

the way Saville could assimilate the most complicated matter, chew it up, turn it around and deliver answers in no time flat, he seemed then not to have the foggiest notion of what she was talking about.

He confirmed her suspicion. 'Trial?' he queried.

'My three-month trial for this job. The job of assistant PA. Annette said, when you didn't get chance to interview me, that she was to take me on on a three-month trial basis.'

'Ah, yes,' he agreed. And she could have thumped him because, having worked herself up into a lather before she could ask her question, that 'Ah, yes' was about the only answer she got. Mutiny entered her soul. She felt sorely tempted to walk out there and then. 'I must say you're very good at what you do,' he added belatedly—just as if he had read her mind.

Hogwash! She stayed—purely because something, and she was blessed if she knew what it was, seemed to be compelling her to stay. Without another word she resumed work.

An hour and ten minutes later, miraculously, it was all done. Edney stretched her back and shoulders where she sat, and realised she didn't feel cross or mutinous any more. She supposed she must have worked it out of her system, and turned in her seat—to find that Saville was watching her.

'That's the lot,' she informed him. But, eyeing the pile of written work he had produced, 'That is, unless you want any of this…'

'You don't think you've worked hard enough these past two days?'

She loved the light in his dark eyes, felt warmed by it. Saville was teasing her! 'Now that you mention it,' she replied demurely and, feeling laughter bubbling up inside her, she turned back to the table, squaring everything up before getting to her feet. 'What time should I set my alarm for the morning?' she queried, laptop secure and ready to return to her room.

'We'll leave the hotel at nine,' Saville replied.

'I'll say goodnight, then,' she offered evenly, suddenly aware that she was starting to feel confused. This was business, she knew she should go, but—she didn't want to, not yet.

She walked by him, her goodnight unanswered. 'Edney!' His voice stopped her. She didn't turn. She felt she was going out of control. If she was feeling loss of control, she didn't want him to see it. She waited. 'Er...' It was unlike him to be hesitant. He was the most decisive person she knew! 'It's early yet,' he added casually. 'We never opened the wine. The least I can do, after your efforts, is to offer you a drink.'

She checked her watch, but was more interested in seeming as casual as he than in finding out what time Saville called 'early'. 'I think I'd rather enjoy a glass,' she accepted, turning back, placing her laptop down and moving towards a chair a yard or so from where he stood.

Somehow, though, her recent accident-prone abilities reasserted themselves. And, when there was not so much as the slightest ruck in the carpet, she missed her footing. She would, she was positive, have corrected her trip before she hit the floor or wall. But she didn't have the space, because Saville was using it!

Not only that, but, his reactions immediate and spontaneous even as he moved to block her, his arms came up to save her. She collided into him. 'For my next trick...' she gasped, looked up into serious dark eyes, and added, 'Sorry—what was I saying about being accident-pr....' Her attempt at humour fizzled out. The look in Saville's eyes was serious still. But there was something else there too. Something she couldn't quite fathom.

'No!' he muttered, almost as if he was having some kind of battle within himself.

'No?' she questioned, her heart suddenly pounding, for Saville still had his arms about her and, crazily, she had an idea that he was reluctant to let her go. 'No—as in…?' she queried huskily.

He took a long-drawn steadying breath, half released her, then, involuntarily it seemed, pulled her closer up to him again. 'No—I'm not going to kiss you,' he said softly, making her heart leap.

She swallowed. 'Which is just as well,' she answered chokily, 'because I wouldn't dream of letting you.'

His head came down, and their lips met. It was utter bliss. She felt his warmth and a need to be that little bit closer still. She took a tiny step forward. Saville groaned, his kiss deepening.

He broke his kiss, looking down at her. She didn't want to move. She hoped he would kiss her again. 'That—er—was heady wine,' she managed—as a kind of aid towards them parting amicably, neither of them having imbibed a drop.

'You're more heady than any wine, Miss Rayner,' Saville murmured, and, his head coming nearer, Edney got her wish when again he kissed her.

And again it was wonderful. Edney gave him her lips freely, responding with every pulsating part of her when his kisses deepened.

She felt as if her heart was going to jump right out of her body when gently he began to caress her. For ageless minutes he kissed her, his warm touch thrilling her. Then, tenderly, his right hand captured her left breast. She felt the warmth of his palm on the outside of her shirt, moulding, caressing, his fingers finding the hardened peak.

She clutched onto him when his expert fingers began

to unfasten her shirt buttons. He halted. 'You seem shy,' he teased.

She loved his teasing. 'You—um—don't,' she smiled dreamily, and to show just how shy she was, she stretched up and kissed him, though that soon changed to him kissing her. Breaking away, Saville then traced tender whispers of little kisses behind her ear and down the side of her throat, both his hands on her back now, under her shirt, making a nonsense of her as they caressed her overheated, on-fire body.

He kissed her again, long, lingering kisses, unhurried, heart-catching kisses—and after a blissful while he began to move with her towards the bedroom. It seemed to Edney, in her luxuriating state, that it was the best idea he had ever had.

She had never been as far as a man's bedroom door before, but now that part of her which previously would have long since called a halt to such proceedings was silent; Edney was not really thinking any more. All she knew was that this—being in Saville's arms—was what she had been born for. She was on fire for him. To be made full and complete love to by him, with him, was what she wanted.

Though, maybe because of that hint of shyness he had picked up in her before, Saville halted with her at the bedroom door. And, kissing her, oh, so tenderly that she thought her heart would melt, he breathed, 'I want you, Edney. I want you to stay with me until morning.'

There was a question there. She answered it with a kiss—but, because she didn't want him to be disappointed in her, she felt honour-bound to tell him, albeit on a husky whisper, 'I want to stay, but...'

'But?' he questioned gently, hearing every word, every nuance.

'B-but—I've heard th-that it isn't always—er—so... That you might not enjoy...' She wished she hadn't started. Saville didn't seem to have a clue what she was talking about. 'I'm sorry,' she apologised softly, stretching up to kiss him.

'I'm enjoying everything so far,' he teased her softly. 'What might I not enjoy, Edney?'

Again she loved his teasing. 'The f-first time,' she got out at last.

He stilled, holding her a little way away from him. 'The first time—for us?' Apparently he needed clarification.

Edney gave it to him as, smiling shyly, she said, 'The first time for me.'

That was when she saw Saville move his head from side to side, as though trying to push through some fog. She went to kiss him; he pulled out of range. He wanted more clarification than that, it seemed. 'Are you saying that you have never been to bed with a man, any man, before?'

'Does it matter?' she asked. 'I mean, I know... That is, I'm not so naive that I'm not aware that it might be...' Her voice tailed off when Saville let go his hold on her—and took a step back. 'It *does* matter?' she questioned. And didn't receive any answers when Saville, save for his arms dropping away from her, just stood there, as if not believing any of it. She stared at him, puzzled, the one striving to push through fog now. 'I don't understand. I'm hanged if I do,' she protested. 'Half my adult life I've been slapping down men who seemed to have only one thing in mind—to take my virginity—so it can't be so bad as all that...'

'Go to bed, Edney!' Saville cut her off, a muscle seeming to jerk away in his temple.

'Go to bed?' She was astonished, but, even if she did desire the swine like crazy, she was intelligent enough to see Saville Craythorne, the changeable, emerging. 'I'll be damned if I'll go to *your* bed!'

With that—though wanting with all she had for him to come after her, to call her back in that gentle tone would have done it—she went.

He neither came after her nor called, and just then, even while she was on fire from sharing experiences with him that she had shared with no other—Edney felt she hated him.

CHAPTER SIX

EDNEY did not sleep well. How could she? She had been on the verge of the most tremendous happening in her adult life, and he—he had told her, 'Go to bed'!

She did not need an alarm call on Sunday morning but was up, showered and dressed long before their nine o'clock departure time. Bearing in mind Saville's changeable nature, Edney had no idea what sort of a mood he would be in when she saw him. But a girl had her pride. Bubbles to it. Was she such a chameleon that she had to suit her mood to his? To blazes with that! Whatever she was feeling inside he was never going to know about it.

With her weekend bag in one hand, her shoulder bag secure, she left her room at two minutes to nine, determined to be pleasant but aloof. She held her head up high, though she was very mindful of where she was walking—it would be great if he opened his door just as she got there and she pitched headlong in, wouldn't it?

She rapped smartly, efficiently, at his door. Saville opened it. Her heart thundered. Her mouth smiled, her eyes fastened on a point near his right ear. 'May I come in and get the laptop?' she requested with cool pleasantness.

'I've got it here,' he replied evenly, and, turning, gathered it up with his luggage from down by the door.

To her mind he was clearly stating that last night's lovemaking had been one huge, regrettable mistake and that he didn't want her anywhere near the inside of his suite again.

He should be so fortunate! She might be jelly-like inside, but she'd hammer the daylights out of him if he tried any of that 'No—I'm not going to kiss you' malarkey again. Though, as she favoured him with her best aloof look, the one he favoured her with, just before she turned about prior to heading for the lifts, was more killing than kissing.

She was glad when their plane landed in London. Conversation on the flight out had been sparse—on the return flight it was non-existent. Indeed, so non-existent that when the time came for them to go their separate ways she was determined that he could go and take a running jump before she'd open her mouth to bid him goodbye.

All she wanted to do then was to get to her car and get away from there. She flicked him a cool glance—and found that he did have something to say to her after all.

Though she could well have done without his lofty 'Thank you for your services,' as he gazed idly down at her.

Well, that put her in her place! Arrogant swine! Edney almost told him there and then to stuff his job. But that something, that indefinable, wish-she-knew-what-it-was something, held her back.

'It was nothing,' she answered sweetly—pick the bones out of that—and didn't miss the chips of ice forming in his eyes. Then, as he turned abruptly in one direction, she turned in the other.

She drove home wanting to cry, and positively hated Saville Craythorne that he could make her feel like that. Who else was to blame! She just wasn't the crying sort! So why did she still want to work for him?

She had never been more relieved than she was when she went into work on Monday morning and found Annette already there. It wasn't that Edney minded being overworked, it was that, just then, she preferred to have as few dealings with Saville as possible.

'How's your mother?' she asked Annette at once.

'Still in hospital, but making a good recovery,' Annette answered with obvious relief. 'The poor dear has fractured her wrist, and has a few other complications, but, all being well, they're talking of allowing her home on Saturday.'

'Oh, I'm so glad,' Edney replied warmly.

'So am I—though I'm afraid I'm going to have to take a week's holiday next week—I feel I'd like to be there to keep an eye on her.'

'You, er, certainly won't want to leave her on her own until you've checked that she can cope while you're at the office,' Edney smiled. Oh, perish it—it would be just her and *him* next week!

'I've no doubt that you'll cope admirably,' Annette assured her. 'I'll be on the other end of the phone if you need me. But, with Saville out of the office from Tuesday to Thursday—when the Milan deal is scheduled to be signed and sealed—your only problem is likely to be the board meeting on Friday, when you'll have to take the minutes.'

Oh, grief! Scared stiff inside at the very idea, Edney managed to hold her smile. From what she had heard of the meeting so far—she'd been happy to listen since she was not to be involved, or so she'd thought—it would be one of those extremely exacting meetings for everyone concerned—the minute-taker included.

'I'll have to see I get a good night's sleep a week on Thursday,' she offered lightly—knowing in advance she was unlikely to sleep a wink!

Thankfully she didn't have time to dwell on anything but the job in hand that Monday. So far she had seen nothing of Saville, but she knew he was in the next-door office, and, while she refused to look up when the door was open, she heard his voice when Annette went in to see him from time to time.

For herself, Edney was loath to go in to see him. But, since the work she'd done in Copenhagen was out of the printer, and many copies made for the eleven o'clock meeting, there was nothing for it—as she knew he would want to run his eyes over everything first—but to go into his office. She knew that even though she'd been at her desk for some while, she was looking closest to her best; she needed to, her pride wouldn't have it any other way.

She stood up, squared her shoulders, and, paperwork in hand, went over to his door. Refusing to swallow, she tapped lightly and opened the door. He didn't look up. She was glad about that—she, who had long since given up blushing, felt her skin burn.

'I think that's the lot,' she murmured with prim efficiency.

His phone rang. 'Answer that,' he ordered crisply.

Yes, sir, no, sir, shall I blow on your coffee, sir? Edney fumed. So, all right, he didn't want to be disturbed, but... 'Mr Craythorne's office,' she said pleasantly down the phone.

'That's Edney!' Felix Stevens exclaimed.

He was all she needed! 'Did you want to speak with Saville, Felix?'

'I was going to ring you later—you've cut short my joyful anticipation.'

Oh, heck. Edney was suddenly made aware by the impatient grunt that came from Saville that—clearly a man with no time to waste or he'd have answered the phone himself—he had been alerted to the fact that his cousin was calling him—and that he was prepared and waiting to take the call.

'I'm—er—a little busy right now,' she said quickly.

'Not too busy to go out with me again, I hope?'

Oh, help! Felix was piling on the charm and seemed

to have all day. She almost said that she'd go out with him, in order to be able to pass the phone over to Saville. But that would be silly. She took a deep breath—and did what had to be done.

'I'm sorry, Felix. I like you very much, but I don't think I want to go out with you again so soon.'

Felix was still using words like 'utterly devastated' when Saville, without a please or thank you, took the phone from her. He did not immediately get into conversation with his cousin, however, but, shooting Edney a cool glance, he addressed her coldly, 'I'm glad to see you're getting some sense at last!'

Lofty pig! Her temper, ever primed where he was concerned, or so it seemed to her, soared again. Oh, to hang one on that firm, aggressive-looking jaw! 'I'm learning all the time!' was the best she could do—which, she owned, when turning smartly about she went back to her desk, was hardly the most cutting retort of the year.

Thankfully, she was too busy to fret over the fact that there was never the right stinging, squelching, cutting remark around when you needed it—though, in her view, it would have to be an extremely brilliant kind of rejoinder to make S. Craythorne Esq squelch.

Edney was glad when five o'clock came around, though it was twenty past before she left her office. There was a pleasant surprise waiting for her in the car park, however, in the shape of her stepbrother. The car park was less than half-empty, and as she crossed it she at once spotted Miles standing by her car.

'Miles!' she beamed, aware that he occasionally came to London for a business meeting, and as ever, always pleased to see him. They greeted each other affectionately with a hug and a kiss, and Miles confirmed that he was in London on his firm's business. 'Have you time to come home with me for a quick dinner?' she urged.

'I'm meeting some colleagues later,' he replied reluctantly. 'The thing is, though, Edney, I was a bit disappointed not to see you yesterday.'

'Knowing you were coming to London today?' she queried. 'What's wrong, Miles?' she asked him worriedly.

'Not a thing!' he exclaimed, and with a bashful kind of grin he went on, 'In fact, everything couldn't be more perfect—Lettie's agreed to marry me!'

'Miles!' Edney squealed, and just had to give him another hug. 'Oh, I'm so pleased. When do I get to meet her?'

'That,' Miles replied, 'is why I wanted to see you. I need a favour.'

'Name it,' she obliged happily, and learned that yesterday Miles had told his father and her mother that he was engaged to be married—and nothing was to be done but to introduce Lettie to them this weekend.

'They were so insistent that I felt I had to agree—your mother was quite upset, actually, that I hadn't said anything about Lettie before. Anyhow, I said I'd take Lettie to tea on Saturday—but Lettie, dear love, she's so shy; I'm sure your mother will terrify her. So, I wondered if you wouldn't mind coming too? You know, ease the pressure a bit.'

'Of course I'll come,' Edney said straight away. Her father wasn't going to like it, but, she decided, 'I'll go down for the weekend.'

'That'll put your mother in a good mood,' Miles murmured.

They parted warmly and, never more pleased for her beloved stepbrother, Edney drove home to find that her father was not so upset at her news as she had thought he might be.

'You've got some little plot of your own planned for this weekend, haven't you?' she accused.

'I don't see why you should be the only one to have some fun!'

Fun! What fun did she have? She'd worked like blazes all last weekend! Then Edney remembered the parties she'd been to. She supposed anyone else might think them fun. And, in all honesty, she also supposed she had enjoyed some parts of those parties, but... Suddenly she thought of Saville—restlessly she pushed him out of her mind.

'Mrs Andrews?' she questioned. Adding quickly, 'You're looking shifty!'

'Rot!' Her father cleared his throat and then, to her utter astonishment, revealed that he did sometimes, well, very often really, take morning coffee and sometimes afternoon tea with Blanche Andrews, and that during one of these afternoon sessions they had discussed those bargain long-weekend holiday breaks which were so often advertised. 'We—er—decided we might quite well like to try one.'

The old rascal! 'You're going this Saturday, aren't you?' she accused dryly.

'Friday, as a matter of fact,' he admitted, 'Coming home Monday.'

'I'm sure you'll have a lovely time.'

'You don't mind?'

'You deserve some fun,' she answered gently. Despite the tug-of-love that had gone on in her childhood, he had been a superb father and she loved him dearly.

Later that evening she telephoned her mother. They discussed Miles's engagement and Edney said she would be visiting this Saturday, if that was all right. 'I missed you last weekend,' her mother confessed. Edney went to bed that night knowing that she had two very nice parents.

Saville came from his office to where Annette and Edney were working several times on Tuesday but, save for acknowledging that she was there, he had nothing to say to Edney. It was the same on Wednesday. Any euphoria she had felt at her stepbrother's engagement, and the fact that her father seemed to be having a more social life, had died down, and that new-found restlessness began to enfold her again.

On Thursday, Edney, while still restless, had something else to think about when the ward sister of the hospital rang Annette after the consultant's rounds to tell her that her mother could leave hospital on Friday. It was clear Annette wouldn't be able to come to work tomorrow!

'I'd better go and see Saville,' Annette said a trace anxiously as she went by Edney's desk. In her agitation she left the door ajar.

What Annette said Edney didn't quite make out, but there was no mistaking Saville's bracing, 'Of course you must have tomorrow off.' She heard more of Annette's lighter tone, and then Saville was saying, 'While you must know you are invaluable to me, Annette, I've every faith in Edney's ability to cope in the short time you'll be away.'

Edney felt inordinately pleased. He had every faith in her ability to cope! While she wouldn't mind at all having half as much confidence, Saville's overheard comment warmed her for the rest of that day.

Matters, however, took a decidedly chilly turn at lunch time the following day. The postal delivery seemed to be bigger than ever that Friday, and Edney began to feel swamped by having to do what she could of Annette's work, complete her own work—and be at Saville's beck and call the whole time.

Not that she had the remotest intention of complaining. Instead she decided to use her lunch hour to do some catching up. She was busy at her computer at a quarter past one, when Saville strode into her office.

'On a diet?' he queried shortly, referring to the fact she was not at lunch, his glance flicking over her slender figure.

She resented the suggestion. While she curved nicely in all the right places, she was naturally slim and lucky enough to never have to diet. 'I'll get a sandwich later,' she replied primly, then saw his glance go to her over-loaded 'in' tray.

'Looks as though you'll be working all day Saturday *and* Sunday,' he commented—and she had an awful feeling that he was needling her for some reason. Perhaps her prim reply had niggled him.

'No way!' she answered. If she had to work until mid-night that night, so be it, but for Miles's sake, not to mention his fiancée, Lettie, she just had to be in Bristol by teatime tomorrow.

'No way?'

Oh, grief. Saville sounded as if he had taken exception to her flouting his 'be available for work at all reasonable times' rule. But, hang it all, she'd worked most of last weekend! What did he want—blood?

She knew she could have explained, and in view of his understanding of Annette's problems Edney realised he would have been understanding of why she was so adamant too. But belligerence entered her soul; why should she explain anything? It wasn't as if he was ac-tually asking her to work, was he?

'No way!' she repeated stubbornly—and I love you too, she fumed angrily as he strode on to the outer door, went through and closed it after him with a determined thud.

And that was when Edney's safe and secure world started to fall apart. For, with enlightenment that made her gasp, she knew at this precise moment that was ex-actly what she did do. She—loved—Saville Craythorne!

'Oh, no!' she cried aloud, every instinct, every part of

her, rushing to let her know what complete and utter folly it was. What a total fool she had been to allow herself to fall in love with him.

Allow? There had been no allow about it. Had she been aware of what was going on within her, then she might, conceivably might, have been able to take some avoiding action—though she doubted it. But she hadn't been aware. This love that burned in her for Saville had crept up on her without her knowing.

She had no idea when it had started. All she knew was that it was there. It was no use trying to pretend that because she didn't want to love him, love him she did not. It was there—and wouldn't go away. She loved him, was in love with him, and had been for an age. And, having at last realised what it was that made her so trembly inside, what it was that made her so emotional, excited, angry, cross—not forgetting as soft as butter about him sometimes—she had to accept the pointlessness of wishing it would go away. It would not; it was far too deep-rooted for that.

Edney was still sitting in a stunned daze when, entering through her office, Saville returned from lunch. She kept her head down, hoped with all she had that she hadn't gone scarlet and dared not look up.

She had no *intention* of looking up until she had some sort of control, but that was before Saville placed a plastic container of sandwiches on her desk. Somehow—she barely knew how—she was able to keep her eyes veiled as her head jerked up.

However, this was one of her soft-as-butter moments. 'Oh, Saville,' she said huskily. 'For me?'

His glance raked her face. 'Can't have you fading away,' he replied, his tone much more pleasant than it had been. Then, his glance going to her barely reduced 'in' tray, he asked, 'Do you need any help?'

She knew he was saying if she needed another pair of

hands to get in touch with Human Resources. But it seemed a point of honour that she coped on her own. 'It won't take me long to move this lot.' She stretched the truth a mile, loving him in this kinder, more approachable mood. And, perhaps because of her discovery of how she felt about him, and suddenly wanting to be friends with him, she smiled and added, 'Truly, there'll be no need for me to come in tomorrow.'

For a moment her smile wavered, when a degree of coolness seemed to enter his eyes. But his tone was even, pleasant still, when, to her surprise, instead of continuing on to his own office, he stayed to enquire, 'So what's so important about this weekend that *no way* can you work?'

Oh, dear, had she been too adamant about that? She wanted to make it better. She couldn't bear that the hostility between them should be there when she left that evening. Somehow she needed some glimpse that he did not exactly hate her to help her get through the next two days when she wouldn't see him.

'I'm sorry,' she apologised. 'Normally I wouldn't have a problem working—were it necessary,' she qualified. 'But I've arranged to go away for the weekend.'

Watching him, Edney experienced a heightened awareness of his moods. He was not happy, she could tell. She looked away from him, down to her desk. Oh, heck!

Then she was startled out of her feeling of wretchedness when, bluntly, Saville enquired, 'With the man you couldn't keep your hands off in the car park last Monday?'

Her head shot up, her mouth falling open. 'I didn't see you in the car park last Monday!' she gasped.

'From the way you were carrying on, I doubt you saw anyone but the man you were trying to make a meal of!'

'Oh, come on!' In an instant she was in arms. To

blazes with loving him! Okay, so she had skirted round Saville's bedroom door, but she wasn't having him belittling her—making out that she was like that with every man she knew. To the devil with parting on bad terms come the end of the day—she'd live with it! 'Yes, I'm seeing Miles again tomorrow, and why wouldn't I? He...'

'Please yourself what you do!' Saville grated. 'Though it might be an idea, *before* it gets to bedtime, to let him into your little secret!'

'You louse!' she flew at him, outraged, on her feet and wanting to pummel his head in. She knew full well that Saville was referring to her letting him know—at almost the last moment—that she had never been to bed with a man before. But that was special between him and her, and she felt she hated him that he could denigrate it so. 'Just because I hugged my stepbrother when he—' she went on hotly—but was stopped before she could go any further.

'Stepbrother?' Saville cut in sharply. 'That was your stepbrother?'

'Yes, it was. And I'll—'

'You seem to have a very close relationship with him,' Saville chopped her off again harshly.

'I have!' she snapped. 'I happen to love him very much, and...'

'*That* was obvious!' Saville rapped, and, his jaw jutting aggressively, he rasped, 'Does he know just how eager you were to climb into my bed last Saturday?'

How she stopped herself from hitting him then, Edney didn't know. 'We all make crass judgements from time to time!' she seethed loftily. This was no longer an office matter. It was personal. But should he dismiss her—then she didn't give a damn!

'Don't we, though!' Saville agreed nastily. He continued acidly, 'Let's hope *Miles* doesn't judge *you* too harshly when, getting into his bed, you tell him, "Funny, it was nearly somebody else's bed last Saturday."'

'Louse is too good a name for you!' Edney yelled. 'And Miles and I don't have *that* sort of relationship. I—' She broke off, suddenly near to tears. It was a humiliation she did not need. Abruptly she turned her back on him, fighting for control, taking deep shaky breaths.

She heard a muttered curse, followed by something that sounded like a groaned, 'Oh, don't cry!' But she was so het up she couldn't be sure. Then suddenly she almost jumped out of her skin when Saville, somehow close behind her, caught hold of her by her shoulders and held her as she fought for control. 'So tell me about this kissing and holding and arms-around-each-other relationship that isn't *that* sort of relationship,' he demanded, his voice tough still, but kinder than it had been.

'It's—n-nothing to do w-with you!' she answered, donning her stubborn hat, albeit a little shakily.

'Yes, it is.'

'How?'

'I've a dreadful feeling I need to apologise—but I'm damned if I'm going to do it if I've got it right and my eyes didn't deceive me,' Saville answered in her ear, and she no longer felt like crying.

'Eat dirt!' she fired, but could do nothing at all about the smile in her voice that had started somewhere down in her toes. 'Normally I would have seen Miles when I paid my usual fortnightly visit to my mother and stepfather in Bristol last weekend.'

'I knew it was going to be my fault,' Saville chipped in, his hands warm on her shoulders, his tone even.

'Of course!' Why should she let him off lightly—she couldn't ever remember having been so upset. 'Because of you—our work—I substituted Copenhagen for Bristol. So when Miles—my much-loved stepbrother—

JESSICA STEELE   113

wanted my support—er...' She started to flounder.
Whether he knew it or not, Saville was stroking her
shoulders with his thumbs and it was making a nonsense
of her.

'Support?' he prompted.

'Well, last weekend, Miles told my mother and his
father about Lettie, and...'

'Lettie?'

'They've just got engaged—Miles and Lettie—and...'
Edney broke off, feeling herself being turned very deliberately around. Saville had his hands on her shoulders
still, and, as Edney looked up, she saw that his expression had lost every bit of its hardness.

'Do I apologise now, or later?' he asked, his eyes
studying her expression.

She smiled up at him. She would forgive him anything. But she was aware through working for him how
he liked everything to be exact, down to the tiniest detail, and felt she just had to clear any other false impression he might be under.

'I didn't know Miles was engaged until Monday.'

'When he met you as you were leaving here?'

'He was in London on business—it was quite natural
that he'd contact me, time permitting. Just as it was quite
natural,' she added, 'that I'd give him an extra hug and
kiss of congratulation when he...'

'When he told you his good news—and asked for your
support?'

There was a question there, but Edney loved him
enough to answer it. 'Miles wanted to know—since none
of us has met his fiancée yet—if I'd go down to Bristol
this Saturday and—well—just be there.'

'His father's against the match?'

She shook her head. 'His father's super. So's my
mother,' she added quickly. 'But she can be a bit—
er—um...'

'A bit of a dragon?' Saville supplied.

Oh, heck. Her love for him fought a battle of loyalty with regard to her mother. Perhaps 'abrasive' had been the word she was looking for. But her love for Saville was new, was tender, and Edney never ever wanted not to be friends with him again.

'Let's say—um—that my stepfather makes a very good St George,' she managed, and felt weak at the knees when the corners of Saville's mouth tweaked at the corners. 'Anyhow,' she went on quickly, 'Lettie's very shy, apparently, so...'

'So your stepbrother feels your support for him and his fiancée is vital when he takes her to meet your family tomorrow,' Saville finished for her.

Edney nodded. 'I have to go,' she stated quietly.

'Of course you do, and I'm every bit the louse you called me for bruising your sensitive soul.'

'I'm sorry,' she found herself saying; it suddenly seemed unbelievable that she had called him a louse to his face.

'See what red hair will do for you,' he smiled, causing her legs to feel like so much water. 'You're lovely,' he murmured softly, and placed the lightest of kisses on her mouth. All Edney was capable of doing was to stare at him. She thought he was going to kiss her again—hoped that he would. But suddenly the phone in his office rang. Unhurriedly his hands fell away from her shoulders. 'We'd better get on with some work,' he decreed.

Edney drove home later than usual that evening, knowing that she had done some work—indeed she'd stayed late to clear the backlog—but she had very little memory of it.

Perhaps it was just as well that her father was not at home that evening. For, having popped a pie in the oven, Edney only realised how much her thoughts were centred solely on Saville when a smell of burning reached

her nostrils. Her father would most certainly have spotted she had something on her mind. She dined on beans
on toast.

Her head was still full of Saville when she drove to
Bristol the next day. Lettie was a pretty, gentle kind of
girl, and it was plain to Edney, who knew him well, that
her stepbrother adored her. She drifted off again; oh, to
have the merest fraction of that kind of adoration from
Saville!

The weekend went well and Edney drove home again
on Sunday, starting to be aware that she was going to
have to snap out of her daydreaming state. Saville was
never going to love her, even a tiny fraction, so she had
better start thinking of something else.

He was still in her head when she let herself into her
home. Annette would be away all this week, and so too
would Saville be, on Tuesday, Wednesday and
Thursday. It was a bleak prospect.

Though Edney cheered up when she thought of tomorrow. She would see Saville again tomorrow. She was
still feeling uplifted by that thought when she went upstairs and began getting ready for bed.

Her uplifted spirits wavered a trifle, however, when
she recalled how changeable he could be. Just because
he had changed from being a brute to a kinder man, a
man who had told her, 'You're lovely', and had lightly
kissed her on Friday, it by no means meant that he would
not have returned to being a snarling brute the next time
she spoke to him.

Edney was about to get into bed when she heard the
telephone start to ring. She checked her watch. Eleven-
thirty. Who in creation would ring at this time on a
Sunday?

Most likely her father, she decided, having a late night
for once. She went quickly down the stairs to answer
the phone. She did so hope that things had gone well

this weekend, but, if he was in one of his cross-patch moods, he wouldn't give a button what time it was or whom he disturbed.

She lifted the receiver, wanting only that her father should be happy. 'Hello?' she enquired tentatively—and waited for her father to tell her what was wrong.

'You took your time answering,' said a voice that was most definitely not her father's, but was one that made her heart leap.

Saville! Joy spread rapidly through her. She opened her mouth to speak, but no sound came. She swallowed, gathered what sense she could find, and knew then that what she must do above all else was conceal the utter bliss it was to hear Saville on the phone.

'I was just going to bed!' she exclaimed in a weak attempt at being scandalised to be summoned at this hour. It was the best she could do. He didn't answer— that was unlike him, she pondered. 'Did I forget something?' she probed. Then she heard his superb voice again.

'Do you remember that conversation we had about you being available at all reasonable times?'

Conversation? Her memory of it was that he'd bossily *told* her what was what, and she had merely listened. 'You want something typed?' Gone half past eleven on a Sunday night was *reasonable?*

'I want you to come and collect me—apparently I can't drive.'

Something was very odd here. 'You don't—sound drunk,' she commented carefully.

'Drugged—sedated,' he replied—and Edney nearly had heart failure on the spot.

'Where are you?' she enquired urgently, striving hard not to panic.

'Hospital!' came the reply, and after telling her which

hospital and what his room number was he said, 'I've had enough of it—come and get me.'

Edney didn't have to think about it. Whether she collected him and took him where he wanted to go was beside the point. If he was in hospital she wanted to be there—she wouldn't rest until she'd seen him. And he had just invited her.

Despite being panic-stricken, Edney found her crisp, efficient assistant PA's voice. 'I'm on my way,' she answered him calmly—and a very short time later was!

CHAPTER SEVEN

ALL the while, as Edney sped to the hospital, she fretted about Saville's condition. Was it serious? Was it life threatening? They didn't admit you into hospital unless it was serious, did they? She couldn't bear it! She choked on a dry sob and made desperate efforts to get herself together.

She was still searching for control when she reached the hospital, which was some way away. By the time she had gained admittance and hurried to the room number Saville had given her, she felt tense enough to fracture at any moment.

Edney found the door she was looking for. She went straight in. The light was on and, given that Saville seemed to have lost some of his usual colour, it was a relief just to see him. He was lying awake on top of the bed, dressed—if the exposed long length of leg from the knee down and glimpse of his chest were anything to go by—only in a hospital robe.

'So, what happened to you?' she questioned, her casual tone belying the mad dash it had taken to get there so quickly.

'What kept you?' he asked sardonically.

'I can go again if you like,' she answered, her eyes assessing him. Albeit he looked a shade quiet, not his usual self, she could see nothing—apart from that small loss of colour—to denote what was wrong with him.

He seemed to study her for a moment, then remarked, 'You must be one of the few women who look as terrific without make-up as with it.'

'Now I know what's wrong with you—you've been

118

hit on the head!' she replied. In addition to her insides playing up over him, her heart was somersaulting because he thought she looked terrific—to apply make-up after his phone call had never occurred to her.

'As a matter of fact, I have,' Saville revealed. And when Edney looked a trace blank, he supplied, 'Been hit on the head.'

'You've been mugged!' Oh, my poor darling!

'Cricket ball!' he announced. 'And this time it's all your fault.'

Cricket ball! Ye gods, cricket balls were as hard as iron! 'I can't even play cricket,' she denied, going closer to the bed, her eyes searching his face, his temple, for a bump or bruise.

'It was your fault—with all your talk of a family weekend, I realised, although I'm frequently in telephone contact, that it was quite some while since I'd seen my parents. I...' He broke off and, clearly having had enough of lying there, sat up. 'Come on, let's get going.'

If he thought she was going to spring him out of hospital just like that, then did he have another think coming! 'We're not going anywhere until I know more,' she returned firmly.

'When did you get to be so bossy?'

'It's the company I keep!' She refused to be browbeaten. 'So what happened?'

Saville gave her a fed-up look of dislike, but, since she had the car keys, and he'd have to get the hospital switchboard to call for a taxi, he replied shortly, 'I got hit by a cricket ball, that's what happened. I went to a cricket match with my father and forgot how good the team were. I must have been distracted by something—can't remember what—and, according to my father, I got in the way of a six.' Edney winced inwardly for him. 'Fortunately it had lost a great deal of its velocity by the time it reached me. All I can remember is waking up here. So, now can we go?'

'Have they said you can go?' Edney received an impatient look for her trouble.

'You're being tedious!' Saville rapped with a touch of his old asperity—he was not a very good patient!

'And you're being fractious. I'll go and find a nurse.'

'Don't you dare!' he snarled, grabbing a hold of her wrist.

What could she do? Fearing that Saville was doing himself no good by growing irascible, Edney sat down on the bed beside him. 'Don't get excited—I only want to do what's best for you,' she stated calmly.

'What's best for me is my own bed! And, yes, they've said I can go.'

'If?' she pursued—and received another look of dislike for her trouble.

'If,' he conceded, 'I have someone who can watch me for the next twenty-four hours.'

'Naturally you thought of me?'

His mouth almost smiled—but he didn't let it. 'If I hadn't, they'd have bothered my parents.'

Edney was glad Saville had called her. It was better than getting a call at the office tomorrow saying he was ill—and not able to personally see him to find out how ill.

'Where are your clothes?' she asked, seeking to distract him; she remembered his snarled 'Don't you dare' at the mention of her going to find a nurse. No way was she going to take him out of there until she had seen someone she knew about his case.

'My father took them to his place!' Saville didn't sound very pleased—clearly his father knew him well. Knew full well that Saville would get dressed and get out of there at the first opportunity if he could.

'Then you haven't got a key to get in?'

'My father took my clothes—my keys and wallet he left. They're in the pocket of this robe.'

'You're looking a little pale,' Edney commented gently, looking at him and feeling her heart turn over— she had somehow never expected to see him looking so vulnerable. 'I'll need to see somebody on the staff to find out what medication you might need before we go. Why not lie down again for a minute or two while I go and sort everything out?'

His look said, Like heck, and Edney knew that he'd pass out sooner than admit to feeling a little tired. She also knew that she was in for one almighty battle with him if her enquiries revealed that he had to stay in hospital. But, whatever sedative they had given him, he was having a hard time continuing to fight it.

'Hurry back!' he demanded gruffly.

She would have liked to stay to see that he lay down, but she fully realised the huge concession it was that he was letting her go and find a member of the nursing staff at all!

Edney went quickly, and soon discovered that Saville had suffered a temporary loss of consciousness; while sleep would do him good, he must be checked from time to time to be certain it was sleep and not coma.

'And it's all right for me to take him home?' Edney asked.

'Even if he hadn't signed himself out—I doubt we'd have much chance of keeping him.' The nurse in charge smiled.

Issued with a small bottle of tablets, and with instructions to call if there was the tiniest sign of deterioration in his condition and that on no account must he go to work tomorrow, Edney went back to Saville to find him lying down with his eyes closed.

'Would you prefer to leave it until the morning?' she asked softly.

'Do you want to keep your job?' he gritted, opening his eyes and sitting up.

'Sounds promising,' she smiled, and moved close in case he needed help in standing.

He did not require her help, but got from the bed and stood unaided, tall, proud and, she didn't doubt, not feeling so good. 'Come on,' he clipped, clearly considering he had wasted enough time in such an establishment.

Edney looked down to his bare aristocratic feet. 'Where are your slippers?'

'Haven't got any.'

'You can't go out with bare feet!'

He tossed her a look which plainly read, Just watch me, and, endorsing that no one told him what he could and could not do, he was in the corridor by the time she caught him up.

Save for giving her occasional directions, he was silent on the drive back to London and his apartment, and Edney worried about him. The sooner she got him indoors and to bed, the better.

His apartment was in an elegant old house; it was discreet, genteel—and must have cost the earth, Edney realised, as, barefooted, he stepped over the pavement to unlock the door.

'Can I get you anything to eat or drink?' she enquired, striving quite desperately not to fuss like some demented mother hen as they stood in the large and high-ceilinged drawing room.

'I'm going to bed!' were the words she got for an answer.

'I'll come and help you,' she asserted before she could stop herself.

And witnessed that Saville must be feeling more shaky than he would have her believe when, without protest, he answered 'Suit yourself.'

Not at all certain what her role now was, Edney felt

she would like to sit beside his bed all night to observe
him—how about that for not fussing? She followed him
to his large and airy bedroom.

Saville, having switched on the main light, was already over by the giant-sized double bed and untying
the belt of his robe when suddenly he paused. Turning,
he looked at Edney, his eyes on her uncertain expression.
Then, even as tired as he undoubtedly was, she saw his
mouth twitch ever so slightly before he murmured,
'Close your eyes, Edney—it's not a pretty sight.'

Why did she want to laugh? Even while she felt herself grow scarlet, she wanted to laugh. Abruptly she
turned her back on him. She heard movement, heard the
sound of the mattress going down as he got on it. She
waited a few seconds more to be sure, then turned
around.

Saville was in bed, the robe he had been wearing now
slung over a chair. Edney went over to him; he had his
eyes closed. 'How's your head?' she asked carefully.

'Ever had that sensation you've been hit by a cricket
ball?'

'I can't give you any painkillers for a while,' she told
him regretfully, aware from her talk with the nurse that
he wasn't due any more for another couple of hours.

'There's no need for you to stay,' Saville said.
'Thanks for coming to get me.'

She didn't want his thanks. Neither did she want to
go. But, by the sound of it, she was being ordered to
leave. She placed the small bottle of tablets she had been
given down on his bedside table. 'Will you be all right?'
she asked quietly, and quickly added, 'You know you
can't go to the office tomorrow.'

'I can't?'

He sounded exhausted. She stretched out a hand and,
bending down, placed her palm on his forehead. To her
surprise, his right hand came from beneath the covers

and he placed it over hers. 'Goodnight, little Edney,' he said softly. 'Go home and get some sleep.'

Being in love was a damnable emotion. One minute she wanted to laugh, the next—like now—she felt like bursting into tears. 'Goodnight,' she said chokily, and as he took his hand away she went swiftly from his bedroom, putting out the light as she went.

She made it as far as his front door. But she found it absolutely impossible to leave. Saville had told her himself that he should have someone watch him for the next twenty-four hours. She could hardly do that if she went home—miles away.

There were several sofas in the drawing room—they all looked extremely comfortable. Edney went silently to the drawing room. Choosing a four-seater sofa, she lay down, but knew she wouldn't sleep.

An hour later she went quietly to Saville's bedroom and, making not a sound, opened his bedroom door and tiptoed in. She went noiselessly over to the bed. His face was turned to the moonlight. She stared down at him, loving him with all she had.

She wanted to gently touch him, to tenderly kiss his face, but could not. Instead she concentrated on listening to his regular-even-sounding breathing. But not until she was absolutely certain that his breathing was natural and not comatose did she leave.

Leaving the bedroom door open this time, Edney returned to her sofa. She left it as long as she humanly could, but within the next hour she was back again, taking a look at him.

He had turned onto his other side but his breathing was as regular as before. She stayed listening for a while, and then considered that since his back was towards her, and there was a chair very nearby—plus the fact that she wasn't going to sleep—she might just as well take advantage of the chair.

Edney stayed listening to his breathing, and loving him with all of her heart, until, some long while later, he turned over again and was facing her.

Silently, or so she thought, she got to her feet. She was still checking the face she loved so much when, with his eyes still closed, Saville drawled quite clearly, 'You can share the bed with me if you like, but I have to warn you, Edney—I'm not at my best just now!'

Startled that he knew she was there, Edney continued to stare at him with a mixture of concern and wanting to brain him. This was more like the Saville Craythorne she knew. From somewhere she found an exaggerated sigh. 'And there was me thinking that this was my lucky night!'

She saw his lips move and curve into a smile, and positively ached with her love for him. He still had his eyes closed. Swiftly she left him—but to go only so far as the drawing room sofa she had used before.

She lay down upon it, and this time felt much more relaxed about Saville's condition than she had done. She closed her eyes and fell asleep.

Given that it was the first snatch of sleep she'd had that night, it was no surprise to her that it was daylight and gone seven before she awoke. What did surprise her, though, was to open her eyes and to find a pair of bare masculine legs in her line of vision. Swiftly her glance travelled upwards, past the towelling robe she had shared a chair with, and upwards again, to find that Saville was standing there watching her. Words sprang to her lips to tell him that he shouldn't be out of bed. Saville got in first.

'I thought I'd dreamt that you were still here,' he remarked.

Hurriedly, very aware of her tousled red hair, Edney sat up. 'How's your head?' she asked in her best bedside manner—given he was not in bed but standing, and en-joying her confusion.

'I've just taken a couple of pills.'

'How are you feeling generally?' she questioned, un-consciously brushing her hair away from her face, re-vealing her delicate cheekbones, noting that his colour was back to normal.

Then she realised that as she was studying him so Saville appeared arrested by her. 'You're beautiful!' he exclaimed softly, involuntarily, or so it seemed.

Her heart raced; she looked away from him. 'You're obviously better!' She found a tart note from goodness knew where—never more did she need to hide her feel-ings for him, to keep her feet firmly on the ground. Saville would dismiss her on the spot if he had the small-est inkling of how she felt about him, and she loved him too much never to see him again. 'What time does your cleaning lady come?'

'What?'

He was quicker than that; she knew he was. 'I'd be very surprised if you're the one who keeps this place so immaculately clean, polished and dusted,' she offered dryly, her heartbeat steadying down a little.

'Nine o'clock,' he answered.

'Then I'll be going,' Edney answered, getting to her feet. She still had to look up at him, but felt more able to cope when standing.

'You're supposed to be looking after me!' Saville pro-tested—and again she wanted to laugh. Love? She wished she could fathom it.

'You were all for my leaving once I'd got you home,' she reminded him.

'That was before I decided that, in the interests of being clear-headed for Milan tomorrow, it might be an idea if I followed advice and took the day off today.'

Oh, heavens, he wasn't fit to go to Milan, and to have

the day off had been an order, not mere advice. But, striving hard to appear cool, Edney hid her inner agitation to state, 'Well, just because you're having time off, it doesn't mean that I can.'

'I thought you were meant to watch over me—that doesn't end until around midnight tonight,' he reminded her.

'Mrs... Your cleaning lady will keep an eye on you.'

'Mrs Dean's only here for three hours.'

'I've an office to go to!' Edney protested, love making a nonsense of her again. Why was she arguing? There was nothing she would like better than to spend the whole day—until midnight—with him. Self-preservation? Fear that her guard might slip and that Saville might see her love and know what an idiot she had been? Pride?

She was facing him, and knew from the seriousness of his expression that something heavy was coming. So she was totally unprepared when, quite conversationally, he enquired, 'What sort of a boss have you got?'

Edney felt a grin coming on, and had the hardest work keeping her expression deadpan. 'You just wouldn't believe me if I told you,' she replied solemnly—and very nearly went to pieces when, for answer, it was Saville who grinned.

Utterly captivated, she looked away, but just had to smile when he offered, 'I'll ring him and make it all right for you to have the day off.'

'I've a lot to do.' She rejected his offer.

He heaved a mock sigh—and deliberately delayed her by stating, 'Starting with making my breakfast.'

Edney made him some scrambled eggs and had a plateful herself. Seated at the breakfast table with him, she so wanted to stay that she found she was having to make excuses to herself for leaving.

She washed the breakfast dishes, was surprised when

he picked up a cloth and began drying them, and muttered, 'My word, that was certainly some bump on the head.'

She had to laugh when he muttered back, 'Saucy baggage!'

'Must dash,' she said, not knowing how to save herself from throwing her arms around him.

'In a hurry?'

'Home, shower, change, office,' she itemised.

'And back here to watch me by midday,' Saville took up.

'Seriously—you'll be all right?' she just had to ask. 'You'll come back?'

'Of course,' she smiled. 'You *are* okay?'

'Stop fussing and go to work. You can bring the Milan paperwork and any urgent mail with you.'

Her smile became a grin. A grin which faded as they stared at each other. She didn't know which one of them moved first, but it seemed the most natural thing in the world that she should reach up and that he should reach down.

Briefly their lips met. 'Go,' he said.

'Be good,' she replied, and went.

She drove first to her home, her head in a quagmire. That kiss had meant absolutely nothing. If anything it had been more part of their light-hearted banter than anything. Edney was still feeling shaken, though when, showered and changed into a smart, short-sleeved linen two-piece, she drove to the office.

No sooner was she at her desk, however, than she had a call from his deputy, Winthrop Butler, saying that Saville had been in touch. 'Any problems, give me a ring,' he offered, adding, 'Saville said you'd be taking any important bits of post round to him later this morning; try to keep the load light.'

Edney promised she would. She had intended to, anyway. Her next call was from Saville's cousin. 'My uncle's just rung to say Saville used his head for a cricket bat yesterday and has signed himself out of hospital. You were the driver, apparently.'

'All part of the service,' she said lightly.

'Would you do the same for me?'

'Do you enjoy cricket?'

'Played for the first eleven. The thing is, I thought I'd pop round and check that he's all right. Uncle says he's spoken to him on the phone and he seems fine—but I think I'll go. Anything you need a hand with?'

Edney told him no, but could not help but feel warmed to know that people were concerned for Saville and that help was there if she needed it. Come to think of it, she had Tuesday, Wednesday and Thursday to get through, too, without Saville.

She did not like the thought, and worked and fretted for the rest of the morning. It worried her that Saville had seemed really keen that she should stay with him that day. Despite his healthy colour, was he feeling more ill than he was letting on?

It worried her too that, Saville having phoned his deputy before she had arrived at the office—his brain was clearly still functioning properly—he might decide to ignore the doctor's instructions and come to work anyway.

Panicking, and on the pretext of work, she found his number and rang him. 'How's the head?' she asked when he answered.

'It would be fine if I had a chance to rest!' he complained. 'I've had nothing but visitors all morning. I should have come to the office.'

That was exactly what she was afraid of. 'Your office is coming to you,' she quickly informed him.

'It already has!' Grumpy-sounding toad—she could tell he was nearly back to being his old self. 'Winthrop called here, as did my cousin. My parents have just left, Mrs Dean's spent most of the morning making coffee, and—would you believe it?—I actually had to promise my mother I'd go to bed this afternoon before she was satisfied.'

'Is being a grouch an expected side-effect of your condition?' Edney asked sweetly. My stars, was he a dreadful patient—was he ever!

Silence the other end—oh, Lord, had she overstepped the mark and offended him? That knock on the head had made him touchy, and no mistake. Relief entered her soul, however, when a moment later he promised quietly, 'I'll get you for that Edney Rayner.' And then he demanded, 'What time are you getting here?'

'As soon as I can,' she said, and put down the phone—only then to realise that her pretext of a work query had never got a mention!

Edney knew that she would go and see him. But she also knew that, above all else, she must guard against him seeing how she felt about him. And she would, no mistake about that, but—for goodness' sake—if she didn't see him again today, she wouldn't see him at all before Friday. And she couldn't take that.

At half past twelve, after leaving word with Winthrop Butler's secretary where she would be, Edney left her office. No doubt Saville had a freezer full of food, but, just in case, she stopped to buy some smoked salmon and some salad. It was quick and easy, and if Saville had already eaten her father would think it his birthday if he had smoked salmon on a Monday.

With her heart full of warmth for Saville she resumed her journey, and, leaving her purchases in her car for the moment, took only a folder of the most important pieces of that day's post with her, and the Milan paperwork he had requested, and went and rang Saville's doorbell.

The door was opened almost immediately. Saville had

exchanged his robe for trousers and shirt, and, as well as looking wonderful, seemed good-humoured. 'What kept you?' She bounded his question of last night back at him, hiding her feelings as she knew she must, waiting for another saucy-baggage type comment. It didn't come, so she crossed over the threshold and he closed the door after her. 'You're looking fine,' she offered brightly. 'How do you feel?'

He looked down at her, his face expressionless. 'Never better,' he replied. Was he lying? She couldn't tell.

They moved to his drawing room and she handed him the papers he'd asked for. 'If you're up to it, we can check the post now, or when I've made you something to eat.'

'Do you know—I could get to like this?' Saville murmured, and she knew then that she had been right; his expression gave nothing away but he was in a good humour.

'Don't get too used to it—it's only lunch.'

'Shame about the bossiness, but...' Oh, she did love him so. She looked away. 'Mrs Dean said something about lasagne and salad,' Saville informed her. 'Shall we eat first?'

In the kitchen Edney saw that everything had been prepared. The lasagne was still warm and required very little heating. As a change from breakfast, which they'd eaten in the kitchen, Edney, with Saville's help—since he insisted—carried everything through to his dining room.

Three quarters of an hour later, she was sitting opposite him and enjoying every moment. They had chatted amiably through the meal. 'Have you lived here long?' she enquired conversationally, loving his elegant dining room, loving him.

'About five years,' he answered, and before she could ask another question, he asked 'How about you?'

'Me?'

'You live in a lovely old house—have you always lived there?'

She wanted to talk about him, not her! 'When they split up—my parents—I lived with my mother for a while.' She gave him a very potted version of the wrangling that had gone on.

'But your father wanted you living with him? You're very close to him,' he observed, probably, she realised, because she'd said she could tell her father everything.

'I am,' she admitted. 'When my mother remarried, he created blue murder until he got custody of me.'

'Which was conditional on your mother having you every other weekend?'

Edney looked at him, feeling quite dazzled. Okay, so it wasn't so very difficult, after what she had told him, for him to work that out. But it pleased her immensely that he remembered so much of what she had said.

'That's about it,' she smiled.

Saville looked back at her, a hint of a smile playing around the corners of his sensational mouth too. 'But, even though you're no longer in need of the court's say-so, you still make your fortnightly trips to Bristol?'

'It's not a problem. My mother likes to see me, and...' remembering Copenhagen '...it has to be something very important to stop me going.'

'Will your mother ever forgive me, do you suppose?'

She laughed. Why wouldn't she? She loved him and he was being close to adorable. 'Um—last weekend— Saturday—in Bristol—went very well,' she mentioned, feeling a sudden hurried need to say something, anything.

His eyes roved her face, traces of laughter still there.

'Are you going to Bristol again this weekend?' he wanted to know.

Edney shook her head. It should have been her weekend for Bristol but, 'Two weekends in a row? My father would have something to say about that.'

'I can see you're much loved,' Saville commented.

It was his love that Edney wanted, and the fact that she loved him and that he never would love her, was starting to hurt. 'I'd better get these dishes washed and the kitchen tidied up.' She switched the conversation as easily as she could.

Saville eyed her carefully. 'You wouldn't care to finish off with some cheese and biscuits?' Thankfully he'd accepted, without wanting to know why, that she wished to change the subject—that she didn't want to talk about her family any more.

'I'm not used to eating much more than a sandwich at lunchtime,' she declined. 'I'll get you some, though, if you like.'

'No, thanks,' he answered, adding, 'do you know, I've changed my mind? I'm quite enjoying being made a fuss of.'

She felt so happy then that Edney knew herself in danger of laughing again. Oh, grief, he'd think he'd got a demented hyena on his hands if she didn't watch her step.

'Make the most of it,' she told him primly, 'I'm going back to the office shortly.' And, taking up a couple of used dishes, she made a hasty exit to the kitchen.

She had just about got herself together when Saville, carrying the plates they had used, joined her. 'You're not staying till midnight, as instructed, then?'

Edney stopped what she was doing and turned to scrutinise him. He *looked* all right, but what did she know? 'Do you have a headache?' she asked, her eyes still searching his face.

'No,' he replied.

That needn't mean anything. He could have taken painkillers a few minutes before she arrived. She started to feel worried again, and quite desperately wanted him to cancel his trip to Milan tomorrow—even though she was fully aware of how important it was business-wise.

'Go and take a seat in the drawing room and I'll bring you some coffee,' she suggested. Even as she said this she started to worry if coffee, a stimulant, was something he should be drinking. His look said she was being bossy again. She turned from him. 'I'll wash up.'

He picked up a teacloth and began drying dishes and she felt better again. Whether he was gasping for a cup of coffee or not, she made a pot of tea. Contrary? She blamed it on love. Saville carried the tea into the drawing room and took a seat on a sofa.

Edney opted for a chair, but could not help feeling anxious when, as he drank his tea, Saville sifted through the folder and paperwork she had brought with her. Should he really be bothering his brain with such complicated issues?

She watched him, ready to insert an answer here or there, should he require some information, and tried to keep a lid on her anxiety. But it was no good. The longer he took to study the matter in front of him, so her inner disquiet over him went into overdrive.

'Talking of mothers,' she blurted out, apropos of nothing.

Saville looked up. 'I missed something?' he enquired.

'You gave your mother your word that you'd go to bed this afternoon!' she reminded him, uncaring that she was starting to feel a fool—Saville had three unbearably heavy days in front of him. Four, if you included that mother-and-father-of-all-meetings scheduled for Friday morning.

He took her meaning straight away. But, counter to

her urgent wish that he would, unquestioningly, just get up and go to his bed, his look instead grew faintly incredulous. 'You're not serious?' he asked, disbelief in every syllable.

'I wouldn't break my word to *my* mother,' Edney replied firmly.

'That's moral blackmail!' he accused.

He could call it what he liked—if it worked. 'Please,' she said.

'My mother will never know.'

Edney took a deep breath. 'She will when Felix gives me her number and I ring her,' she murmured, fully expecting to get thrown out for her nerve.

Saville stared at her, his look still disbelieving. Then, suddenly, a devilish light was there in his eyes. He stood up. 'Come on then,' he said.

Automatically, Edney stood up too. 'Where?' she questioned.

There was definitely wickedness there—it was written all over him. 'My dear, Edney,' he drawled, 'if I'm going to bed—you—are coming with me.'

Shaken rigid—she stood rooted, and just stared, her brain seeming to have seized up. 'No!' she gasped, her stomach somersaulting, her heart thundering, her eyes saucer-wide.

'Oh, but, yes,' he assured her, and, stepping forward, he took a firm hold of her wrist. 'We'll go now,' he said, and while she dug her heels into his plush carpeting, refusing to budge, he added. 'Bring the paperwork with you. You can talk me through it while I close my eyes.'

'You...' she began, and suddenly wasn't worried any more—the rat had been playing with her! So, okay, perhaps she had overstepped the mark by threatening to phone his mother. But at least it had got the result she wanted. 'Um—you're—er...' She began to check herself, a small margin of doubt catching her out.

Saville smiled at her then. 'Relax, Edney,' he instructed her gently. 'To comply with my promise I'll lie on top of the duvet, and you can take a chair and sit and read to me.'

That seemed a fair bargain—it wasn't as if it was the first time she'd been in his bedroom with him. Indeed, as she started to gather up the various papers, Edney began to feel quite good about the result she had pushed for.

She was still feeling that way some time later when, her pen flying furiously over paper, Saville dictated note after note. Then there were just two more items to be dealt with, then they would be done.

Edney started reading the first of the two to him, a sick feeling starting to enter her because soon she would have to leave. Could she delay by making him some more tea? Perhaps she could make some sort of a meal for him, for later on.

Saville, suddenly cutting in when she paused after a paragraph, caused her to halt and stare at him. 'You have a very soothing voice, Edney,' he complimented her.

He had his eyes closed. Was it the light in the room, or was he paler than normal? Edney tried not to fret. 'Thank you,' she answered politely, still trying to assess him as, more slowly this time, she carried on reading.

She came to the end of the page and glanced over to him. He wasn't responding with any instruction. Without making another sound, she sat watching him for a minute or so. His eyes were still closed, his breathing even.

Was he falling asleep? Was he, in fact, already asleep? Sleep, a natural sleep, a natural rest, could only do him the world of good, in her opinion. Silently she watched him for another minute. He *was* asleep.

It was a warm day, but, feeling certain that the body temperature dropped in sleep, and fussing though it might be, she looked round for some light covering to drape over him.

She could see none. Though looking at the giant-sized bed she took in that it was covered by an equally giant-sized duvet. Putting her papers down and, without a sound, leaving her chair, Edney approached the bed, stretched down a hand to the duvet—and at once realised she had made a mistake. Saville was not asleep!

In a flash he opened his eyes while at the same time his right hand shot out and grabbed her wrist—pulling her to sit down on the bed beside him.

'You!' she gasped. 'You weren't asleep!'

He looked smug. 'Who's a grouch?' he questioned— and too late she realised she should have taken more notice of his promise, 'I'll get even with you for that', when she had phoned him from the office.

'You tricked me!' she accused, her heart racing—he still had a firm hold of her wrist.

Saville ignored her accusation. 'You call me names, threaten to blackmail me. Not nice, Edney. Now, what forfeit will you pay?'

She looked at him. That devilment was back in his eyes again. She wanted to kiss him, to be held by him. She ached to be held by him. 'You were right, you should have gone to the office. The trouble with you is you're bored and looking for mischief,' she reprimanded him coolly.

'Forfeit!' he demanded, not a bit put off.

She looked at him, happiness bubbling up inside her. 'How about I make you a sandwich?' she offered.

'Not hungry.'

Oh, help her, someone. 'A cup of tea?'

'Not worthy of you.'

'I—suppose—I could—er—give you a little kiss. But you wouldn't like that?' Oh, treacherous heart, wayward tongue, and that need to be closer still to him!

'I would,' he contradicted, devilment still there in his eyes.

'You wouldn't,' protested some very weak, sane part of her that was trying to get through.

His answer was to pull her nearer to him. 'Try me,' he suggested.

She swallowed, knew she was losing it. 'You—um—must lie very still,' she instructed. 'I'm—er—not sure this is very good for you.'

'I'm lying very still,' Saville answered—she didn't trust him.

Or was it herself she did not trust? Because, as she leaned over and their lips met, the thin strand of control she had been striving so hard to hang on to was lost.

His mouth was warm and inviting beneath her own. She raised her head; she paid her forfeit, but with Saville this close, so close, she did not seem able to pull completely away.

Nor, it seemed, did Saville want her to pull away. For perhaps all of two seconds they stared at each other, she making strenuous efforts to hide from him any glimpse of love he might see in her eyes. His eyes showed a gentleness, the devilment and mischief all at once banished.

'Edney.' He murmured her name, and the next thing she knew was just the pure, utter bliss of being enfolded in his arms.

Unhurriedly, he kissed her, his arms holding her. Her heart was hammering. She touched his face. He kissed her throat. She thrilled to his touch. His mouth found hers again, she clung on to him, and for long, wonderful minutes they shared kiss after kiss.

She felt the caress of Saville's tender hands at her waist, and held on to him when his fingers caressed upwards beneath her linen top. His touch was exquisite on the bare skin of her back. And she had not the smallest protest to make when, her bra an encumbrance to his progress, he undid it, his hands making gentle, mind-boggling, tender swathes over her silken skin.

'You're all right, Edney?' he asked.

Somehow she had a vague feeling she should be asking him that question. But just then she had no idea why she should want to ask any such thing.

'Oh, yes,' she answered shyly, and kissed him, and moaned with pleasure when his hands gradually caressed round to the front of her. Unhurried, he captured her bare breasts in his hands. 'Oh!' she whispered.

'I'm not scaring you?' Saville asked softly.

She shook her head and felt an almost overwhelming urge to tell him that she loved him. But somehow she found she had retained just enough sense to know that such an admission would be most unwelcome.

Then she forgot everything, save that Saville was caressing the hardened peaks of her full, throbbing breasts and she just wasn't thinking at all. She wanted to touch him; it became urgent that she did so. With unseasoned fingers she fumbled at the buttons of his shirt—and found that Saville was more than willing to help.

Indeed, as they kissed and clung to each other, she was barely aware of sitting with him on the bed, barely aware of his shirt being disposed of, her top and bra being disposed of. Of where and how her skirt went, she had very little memory.

'Saville!' She cried his name when suddenly discovering that her only covering was her briefs, and his was a similar single item of underwear.

'You're not going to panic on me, are you?' He smiled, his hands caressing her satiny shoulders.

'I wouldn't dream of it,' she whispered, and adored him totally when she felt the bare, hair-roughened maleness of his chest against her breasts as they kissed.

She was not so sure about not panicking, though,

when Saville gently pulled back so he should see more of her. Edney was certain she blushed scarlet as his eyes traced down over her breasts, tiny waist and hips, and back again to the naked full swollen globes of her breasts. He gently touched a finger to darkened tips that just invited a kiss, a caress. And Edney knew the wonder of the moist touch of the inside of his mouth as, in turn, he took the hardened tips and a little of the delicate creamy mounds inside his mouth.

Gently his tongue curved around the tip of her right breast, his teeth taking over to tenderly nibble and light such a fire in her that she was close to crying out her need for him. His mouth moulded her right breast again while, with one arm holding her, his other hand caressed at her left breast.

She clutched on to him, knowing that there was no going back. Nor did she want to. Saville's mouth left her breast and he kissed her deeply, and at last brought her to lie down with him.

Never had she experienced such heightened sensations. He kissed her, lay half over her, their legs touching, intertwining. 'I want you, so much,' Saville breathed.

'I th-think you know that I want you,' she answered shyly. And was kissed.

'Don't be afraid,' he breathed.

'No,' she smiled, and kissed him and clung to him, and with just their single items of clothing separating them she somehow found that, perhaps instinctively, Saville's body was all the way over hers, covering her. She felt his thighs against her thighs, and pulsated everywhere with her longing for him.

Without her known volition, she found that she had adjusted her body somewhat, that she had somehow bent a knee, holding him against her right thigh. A trace of panic impinged on her then. To be with Saville like this,

Saville, the man she loved, was little short of enchanting. To feel his skin, his hard male body against hers, was utter bliss.

But warning bells, unwanted, unneeded warning bells, were starting to go off. Warning bells not for herself, but for him. She wanted him, quite desperately did she want him. So much so, she was having the mightiest struggle to remember why she should be worried about him.

'I…' she gasped hesitantly. And could only love him more that, when she could barely fathom herself what was bothering her, Saville appeared to have picked up from that one word, from her tone, that something was wrong.

'What?' he questioned, seeming to be doing his very best to clear his head so that he might grasp what, if anything, the problem was.

That was when Edney surfaced to realise what worried her. It was his head. His poor head! 'I'm—er—n-not sure about this!' she exclaimed.

'You're—not *sure?*' Saville stared at her, and, when she knew his powers of comprehension were first class, she saw he was having difficulty with her answer.

'I—don't think it's—um—right!' she jerkily tried to explain, and saw that Saville was battling with something—she knew not what. Then she saw the tenderness in his look begin to fade. To her amazement, before she could find the words to explain—forget coffee as a stimulant, what was more guaranteed to overwork the stimulation gland, the adrenalin, than an afternoon of passionate lovemaking?—Saville was rolling away from her.

'Saville?' she questioned doubtfully. He was sitting on the side of the bed, his back to her. She wanted him. Quite feverishly she wanted him. Her need was such that it was getting in the way of what she had to consider was right for him.

Which, while her brain and heart were having the most dreadful time in separating right from wrong, was no aid at all to her in trying to grasp what was going on. She heard Saville quite clearly say, albeit tautly, 'I think the best thing you can do for both of us is to leave!'

Leave! Thunderstruck, she stared at his wonderful broad naked back. She wanted him—he was throwing her out. 'Saville!' she protested.

'Now, right now, wouldn't be a bad time!' he clipped.

Her mouth fell open in shock. He wanted her; she knew he did. Stunned, she stared at the back of his head. She didn't want to leave! She wanted to stay—if not to make love with him—and oh, how she still wanted him—then at least to find out if he was all right.

Suddenly she started to grow terrified that the stimulus of their lovemaking might be having an adverse effect on him. *'Now!'* he repeated harshly.

And that was when her pride arrived, a fierce pride that pushed everything else out of her head. He wanted her to leave! He was throwing her out! How *dared* he? 'Changeable' had she called him? Devil take the hindmost—he was never the same two minutes together. Leave! She couldn't wait to be gone!

Hurriedly she gathered up her clothes, caught sight of her near nakedness—and felt just then that she hated him for the wanton he had made of her. Quickly she got dressed, pride taking her storming to the door.

She didn't look at him again, couldn't look at him again. But for once she found the exit line she needed, when, opening the door, she snapped, 'That was one hell of a forfeit, Craythorne!' And got out of there.

CHAPTER EIGHT

IT TOOK Edney a very long time to get herself back together again—days, in fact. She did not return to the office on Monday afternoon but instinctively headed for her home. Though it wasn't until she saw her father's car on the drive that she realised he was back from his short holiday, and that she was going to have to get herself into more of one piece very smartly.

She discovered on Tuesday that a messenger had delivered the notes and paperwork she had left behind in her haste to decamp Saville's apartment. But there was no personal note from him, just a pencilled instruction on the work they hadn't completed. Though why she expected him to write anything of a personal nature, Edney wasn't sure. He hadn't, she recalled without effort, seemed very pleased with her if that, 'Leave now' was anything to go by.

Wednesday dragged endlessly. But by Thursday Edney was feeling more able to cope. Although each time she thought of how close, how intimate she and Saville had been with each other, she was hard put to it to know how she was going to manage when next she saw him.

It was all right for him, of course. She didn't doubt that he'd been in that situation before. Though she didn't suppose it was every day that, in the middle of making love, he told the—um—responding party, that she'd better leave.

That word 'responding' threw her. She wished she could say that she had not responded. But she had—wholeheartedly! But for her—and it had to be said, belated—remembrance that Saville had suffered a head injury, Saville might have made complete love to her.

She had wondered if her interrupting the—er—proceedings the way she had was the cause of Saville calling a halt to their lovemaking. Perhaps, when—matters—got *that* heated, one wasn't supposed to talk? What did she know? What didn't she?

What she did know was that she was missing him. Even though she wasn't sure how she was going to face him, she was missing him so badly she could barely wait for tomorrow to see him again.

On Friday she dressed in her smartest business outfit, a cool navy skirt and top with white edging. She knew she looked good, and needed to know it. She drove to work with her stomach in knots.

Edney parked her car, spotted Saville's car, and went up to her office. Then found she had to take a deep and steadying breath before she could go in. Anticlimax was her reward when she did enter!

The door between the two offices was open and a quick glance showed that Saville was there and was already hard at work. But so much for her worrying about how she was going to face him or look him in the eye—he didn't so much as glance up.

She went and stowed her handbag. 'Would you come in, Edney?' he ordered, his tone cool and impersonal. Two could play at that game.

Taking up her notepad, she went in. She had intended asking how he was, but it was plain from his manner that he wanted to remember nothing of that time—wanted to remember nothing of a personal nature that had passed between them.

'Good morning,' she said crisply, and hated that pathetic, weak part of her that still wanted to ask how he was.

How was he. Tough, businesslike, cold—and Edney

felt that she hated him because of it! How could he, after the near-naked way they had lain together, dictate this, dictate that, as though nothing had happened!

He stood up, checking his watch, as ever tall, immaculately suited, every inch the businessman he was, and, to Edney, quite devastating. 'I'm off to see Winthrop Butler and a few of the others. I'll leave you to see to the post and lock anything in my drawer that needs my attention.'

'No problem,' she answered calmly, her eyes fixed down on her notepad as if glued.

'Don't forget the meeting starts at ten!' he reminded her—unnecessarily in her opinion. She was the one who'd sent the notices out!

'I'll be there at five to,' she replied evenly.

Without another word, he went. And, feeling as if she had been firmly put in her place—at the very least having received a very clear message: Forget you were ever on my bed—I must have been more concussed than I realised—Edney, feeling as though she'd been slapped, gritted her teeth, tried not to cry and tore into some work.

It was again a matter of pride that she was in the conference room well on time. Saville and Winthrop were last to arrive. She saw Saville glance at once to where she was supposed to be, and guessed she'd have been mincemeat had she dared to not be there.

That was the only acknowledgement he made of her presence—and she was hating him afresh. So, all right, she didn't expect him to dance a jig of joy that she was present. Which was just as well—she had a feeling that he regarded her as just another piece of office furniture. But he might have said, Ready? Or something of that nature. Was that expecting too much?

The meeting got under way and Edney didn't have time to think of anything other than the complicated, not to say mind-boggling facts, figures and corporate language that went on for the next two and a half hours.

Then it was Saville's turn to address and close the meeting, and she could only marvel at the way, without pause or hesitation, he summarised all that had gone on.

Quite when her hatred of him went flying out of the window she couldn't have said, but love and admiration were only in her heart, she found, at the effortless way he précised the most complicated of issues. Her pride in him began to soar! All this when less than a week ago he'd been poleaxed by a cricket ball!

She began to wonder if he had fully recovered from that blow to the head. He'd looked so pale, so tired, when she'd collected him out of hospital—less than a week ago. He was winding up the meeting now, and she flicked a glance to him, finding that, though she had been stressed, now, with the more complicated issues out of the way, she was able to relax a little. She loved him so, and could not deny that she felt all soft and tender inside.

He turned her way, still talking, still addressing his audience. What a wonderful job he'd done—what a wonderful person he was. She loved him, oh, how she loved him.

Oh! Suddenly, abruptly, all thought ceased! While everyone had their attention on Saville and what he was saying, he moved his head slightly, unexpectedly, and looked straight at her. And, when in the last half-hour he had dealt with complicated detail after complicated detail without falter, he hesitated then, as his eyes met hers. All at once, in the middle of simply drawing the meeting to a close, Saville looked directly into her eyes—and faltered. Faltered, looked a shade stunned, his brow lifting as if he'd just received some kind of shock.

Oh, no! Edney felt her face go scarlet. Then she immediately broke out into a cold sweat—her emotions exploding in a bomb-burst of utter horror! She knew precisely what had stunned Saville!

He ended his concluding remarks. Edney was on her feet, and—taking advantage of the fact that several of the directors and others were crowding around him and near him—she was out of there. With terror in her heart, she raced to her office, locked her notes in a drawer and, pausing only to retrieve her bag—she was on her way.

Panicking wildly, with no time to wait for the lift, she bolted for the stairs, made the first landing, and, glancing hurriedly back before she went to round the next bend, caught a glimpse of Saville going purposefully, and at some speed, along to his office.

She charged on down, aware that he and some of the board members had a lunchtime table booked at a restaurant. By no chance did she wish to bump into him in the car park as he left.

Edney's head and heart were still in a whirlwind of exploding thoughts and emotions when, having driven out of the car park without seeing Saville again, she suddenly became aware that she had driven a fair way without knowing it, and was, in fact, very close to her home.

Edney pulled into a little-used lane around the corner from her home. She felt bruised, sick at heart and utterly wretched. This was something which, on this rare occasion in her life, she felt she could not share with her father. The pain, the humiliation, went too deep for that.

For remembering Saville faltering as his eyes met hers, that moment as a stunned kind of shock had taken him, Edney knew that he had seen what in that unguarded moment she had made no attempt to hide—that she was in love with him!

Feeling mortified, Edney went over what she knew of him. He was astute, sharp, and he knew women! Without doubt he could read a word, a look, a sigh. And what had she done, when previously she had been at pains to hide from him her true feelings? She had, in that unguarded moment, when his eyes had been elsewhere, been so proud of him, felt so tender-hearted towards him, all her sensibilities going out to him, all her emotions welling up in her, that in the instant when he turned to glance at her her love for him must have been shining out like some beacon! Oh, it was *unbearable!*

Up until today, remembering last Monday afternoon—and she knew she would never forget—any emotion or passion she had shown him could, she felt, be put down to perhaps an awakening of some biological physical need. Lord, how clinical that sounded! But, at any rate, he would know that consenting adults could make love without actual love being involved.

That she was the exception that disproved the rule was neither here nor there to him—until today, when he would have had to be blind not to see that she cared for him. But Saville had no use for her love. He did not want it, and, while she appreciated he was too sophisticated for it to be an embarrassment to him, once he had got over his shock—that would take less than a minute, she realised—he would take stern steps to deal with it.

Edney wished that she felt better about saving him the bother of telling her not to come in on Monday. She already knew she wouldn't be going back to I. L. Engineering and Design. Knew it for fact. Annette was brilliant at pretty well everything to do with the office—Edney was sure she would be able to decipher her notes.

Annette was far from Edney's thoughts when, an hour or so later, she felt calm enough to continue on her way. She would have to tell her father that she had walked out on her job—before she was pushed out—and crave his indulgence not to question her about it.

When she went into her home, however, it was to

discover that her father was not in. The phone rang, but for once she ignored it. She did not feel like making polite conversation. And, since she was supposed to be at her office, it would not be for her anyway.

The phone rang several times that afternoon—someone was obviously seriously interested in contacting her father, but she had little idea of where he might be, and, in any case, she still felt too heart-sore to want to answer it.

Her father arrived home shortly before the time she would normally get back from work. 'Hello—you're early!' he exclaimed—and the words to tell him that she had walked out of her job—though sprinted was a more apt description—just weren't there.

'Making up for all that overtime I've worked,' she replied instead. Then she drew a steadying breath to get it all over with. 'Actually...' she began, only her father was speaking at the same time. Respectfully, she offered him the floor.

'I've been—er—out,' he took up, and seemed a trifle hesitant, she thought.

'Having tea with Mrs Andrews?' Edney attempted to make it easy for him, and learned she had guessed correctly.

'Er—as a matter of fact, yes,' he replied. And, with that out of the way, he went on, 'Blanche wondered— and you can say no if you want to—if you'd like to go to her house to dinner tomorrow night?'

Her father wasn't a man to openly show his emotions, but this sounded serious stuff. And to have passed on the invitation at all meant that her father wanted her to accept.

Edney put her heartache to one side and found a smile. 'You'll be there?'

'Of course!' he answered promptly.

'Then I'd be delighted,' she told him and, her heartache refusing to be put to one side for more than a few moments more, added, 'I'll go up and change.'

'And I'll go and phone Blanche.'

With her father clearly in very good spirits, Edney felt a definite reluctance to tell him anything that might mar his mood. So she found another smile instead, and watched him make his way to the hall phone.

The phone rang before he could make his call, however. Edney passed him in the hall as he picked it up. 'It's for you,' he said, holding the phone out to her.

Edney, hoping that it wasn't one of her group of friends ringing up for a chat, went and took it from him. 'Hello?' she said, and nearly died of shock!

'What are you doing there?' questioned a tough voice she knew straight away.

'It's where I live!' she answered on a gasp, and hastily slammed the phone down.

Fortunately her father had disappeared and Edney, her head once more in a whirl, ran upstairs to her room. Saville knew that she loved him—what more did he want?

Choking back a sob, Edney paced her room. To blazes with her being in love with him; he must have considered it highly inconvenient of her to not to have been around for him to dictate his orders to when he returned from lunch.

She tried to drum up hate for him, but could not find the feeling she wanted. He hadn't asked her to fall in love with him, and was probably quite appalled to discover that she had been so stupid. But anger stirred in her heart; there was no need for him to ring her to dismiss her—she'd already got that message.

Her anger faded when it dawned on her, not only because of her business dealings with him, but because of that certain sensitivity she had witnessed in him a couple of times, that to dismiss her formally—perhaps in view of those heated moments they had shared—would not be his way. While he might confirm it in writing, from what she knew of him, she began to realise, he would tell her verbally first.

She changed from her smart suit into jeans and a cotton tee-shirt—and heard the phone ring again. He wouldn't call a second time? Would he?

'Edney!' her father called up the stairs. 'It's for you!'

Her legs felt weak. It wouldn't be him. He wasn't the only one who had her phone number! With her insides all of a swirl, Edney went down to the hall. 'Thanks, Dad,' she said, and as he went on his way she fearfully picked up the phone. 'H-hello?' she said huskily.

'I think we'd better meet!' stated a firm, decisive voice that could only belong to one man.

'I don't!' she returned in no time flat—and, more politely this time, she put down the phone.

Who did he, with his 'I think we'd better meet', think she was? Did he think she'd meekly turn up at some venue just to be told face-to-face, You know that three-month trial? You blew it!

'Was that the same man?' her father came out into the hall to ask.

'My boss,' she explained. Now still didn't seem to be the right time to tell him as much as he should be told. 'We—there was a high-powered meeting this morning...'

'And he sent you home early but is still tying up loose ends,' her father finished for her, getting it completely wrong.

'What do you fancy for dinner?' She changed the subject completely, her father postponing phoning Blanche Andrews until after their meal.

Then he decided that instead of phoning he would pop round to see her. He was away some time. Edney could not have been more glad about that, because it meant that she was the only one in when, a short while later, she heard a car coming up the drive. Looking out of a window, she just could not believe her eyes.

What was Saville doing here? Before he was out of his car she was upstairs in her room. She lay flat on her bed in panic, not wanting to be seen. She heard him ring the doorbell and prayed, since she had not the smallest intention of answering it, that her father would not return until after Saville had gone.

The bell went a second time, a third and a fourth. Long and hard did it ring. Her insides were choked with tears, but there was nothing in this world that was going to make her answer the door. She knew that he would have spotted her car on the drive but, even though he had seen her love for him, that didn't mean she stayed home nights. She was hopeful he would think she was out on the town somewhere. Out with a date.

There was no fifth ring at the door. When Edney heard the sound of his car starting up, so very nearly did her heart stop. It was the end; she knew it. Saville, like the man he was, had tried to speak to her, both on the phone and in person. In his book he had done what he felt he should do. He would not try again.

So convinced of that was Edney that when, five minutes later, the telephone rang, she gave serious thought to answering it. She was more in control now than she had been.

The phone was still ringing when, unhurriedly, she left her room and went down the stairs. The phone carried on ringing—perhaps it was important. Still without haste, she picked up the handset. 'Hello?' she said. And just did not believe what she heard.

For, quite clearly, in a voice that was Saville's and no other's, 'Edney,' he said, 'I love you!' and, as cool as you like, ended his call.

Edney had no recollection of putting down her phone.

She just stood staring at it there on its rest, while her mind refused to function.

Completely staggered, she was still staring at the phone, as if hypnotised, when she heard her father returning. Unable to think, to talk, she fled up to her room only to realise, some ten minutes later, that she couldn't stay there for the rest of the evening—yet neither was she capable of going downstairs and making everyday conversation. Saville just couldn't have said what she thought she had heard him say!

Taking up her bag, and extracting her car keys as she went, Edney went downstairs and into the sitting room. 'Everything all right with Mrs Andrews?' she somehow managed to find just the right note to enquire.

'She's looking forward to tomorrow evening,' he answered, and, spotting her car keys dangling from her hand, asked, 'Going out.'

'Shouldn't be long.'

'I won't wait up,' he quipped.

Edney had been driving for a full fifteen minutes when she suddenly realised that the direction in which she was driving was of Saville's apartment.

Heavens above! She executed a speedy about-turn at the first possible opportunity. What on earth did she think she was doing? Yet, somehow, she was not ready to return to her home, and at the first available parking spot she pulled over and halted her car. He couldn't have said 'I love you'! It was inconceivable that he had declared that he loved her! Yet—she couldn't get it out of her mind.

She went over what she thought he had said again and again. 'Edney, I love you,' he'd said—or something very like it. Seriously doubting her hearing, Edney tried to think of what else sounded like 'Edney, I love you'—but nothing else would fit.

With her insides all of a tremble, she battled to cope

with her feelings for being totally staggered and began to realise that, whatever he had said, he must have said it from his car phone. His home was more than five minutes away from hers. There would not have been time for him to make that call from his apartment.

Which only seemed to confirm that he had known full well, while she had been determined not to answer the door, that she was in!

While she, she didn't know where the Dickens she was. Had she gone mad! Had loving him turned her brain? What she wanted to hear was Saville telling her that he loved her—but he couldn't have said what she wanted to hear…could he?

Edney strove valiantly to think logically—but with her emotions in such an uproar not much of a logical nature was getting through. Had he said it? Did he mean it? Well, she knew the answer to that!

But why would he say it—if said it he had. It was clear that he wanted to speak with her—and she, she rather thought, had made it clear that she did not wish to speak with him.

Had that been it? Fed up with trying to have a conversation with her, he had dropped that bombshell to get her attention? Well, he had that all right!

But—why would he want her attention? Some business matter? Would he do that? Somehow Edney couldn't see him mixing business with things like that. Why, look at him this morning after how close they had been on Monday, after the way they'd been wrapped in each other's arms! Look at…

Suddenly her thoughts were faltering. Was it possible that Saville had been striving to keep business and his feelings for her apart? Feelings? Feelings for her? Did he have any feelings for her? Oh, he desired her—or had—she knew that. But—feelings?

Oh, dear heaven, had Saville actually said, 'Edney, I

love you'? Edney drew a fractured breath and for another five minutes she sat there, pushing at it, pulling at
it—had he said it?—did he mean it?—but was desperately unable to come to any conclusion. Any conclusion,
that was, other than she knew she would never rest again
until she knew for sure. No way could she return to her
home and go to bed until she knew one way or the other.

Saville had phoned her three times and had also visited her home. She had a fear that he might not try again.
She swallowed hard. Because if he was not going to try
again, that then meant she was going to have to be very
brave—and go to see him. Could she be that brave?
Could she?

Edney, after another minute of striving for control,
reached forward and switched on the ignition. Then she
manoeuvred her car and drove quite some way down
that road. Then, on a moment of courage, she executed
a sharp U-turn.

She drove to Saville's apartment, striving not to think
at all. She hoped he was in. Though, as nerves grabbed
a merciless hold on her and she arrived outside his home,
she found that she was hoping that he was not in, that
he had not yet returned.

She stood on the pavement, knowing full well that if
she felt that strongly all she had to do was get back into
her car without bothering to ring his doorbell. But something, some force she could do nothing but obey, was
pushing her forward.

Edney went to his door, stretched out a shaking fore-
finger and rang the bell. She had ready a cool sentence
along the lines of telling him that she'd finished being
available at all hours when the door opened—and she
forgot every word of it.

She owned to being in a quite dreadful state as, tall
and straight, casually dressed and with dark good looks,
Saville stared down at her. 'I—um—I left my scarf here

last Monday!' The unsought lie came blurting from her lips—she hadn't had a scarf!

Saville eyed her steadily, unsmiling, for several moments. And then he said, 'I found it. Come in.'

CHAPTER NINE

SAVILLE ushered her into his drawing room, or at least Edney thought he must have done, because that was where she found herself—standing in the middle of his carpet, with everything in her a mass of confusion; she had no true recollection of getting there.

'Take a seat,' he offered solemnly. There wasn't a smile, so much as a hint of liking her, let alone loving her, about him.

And, too late, Edney suddenly saw that his declaration of love was merely a ruse to get her there. He knew that she loved him, that the only thing that would get her to see him was if he told her he loved her—it was humiliating.

Which left her with very little option but to show him just how completely wrong he had got it. 'I shouldn't have come,' she told him coolly, ignoring his invitation to take a seat and heading for the door.

'Yes, you should!' he answered sharply, moving to block her way.

'No!' she exclaimed, all at sea, a conglomeration of contradictions within herself where everything she had thought she knew of him had been turned upside down. She was unsure if she was protesting at him preventing her from leaving or the fact he was denying her statement that she shouldn't be there. She took a step back— another step forward and they would be touching. Even feeling cold towards him, as she did at that moment, Edney was nervous of physical contact with him.

Saville eyed her steadily, refusing to move out of the way—as if, having got her there, he was determined she wasn't leaving until he'd had his say. He confirmed it. 'There are—things—between us that have to be said!' he decreed.

If he thought she was going to meekly stand there while he castigated her for her unseemly behaviour in daring to fall in love with him, and followed that with some polite—or otherwise—phrase of dismissal, did he have another think coming! She measured the distance between him and the door, trying to calculate her chances of sprinting past him and out of there.

'You'd never make it!' he said silkily—and she hated him, for, by watching her eyes, he had read her mind.

She was extremely tempted, then, to invite him to say what he had to quickly and get it over with. But she had to live with herself afterwards, and in her view she had suffered enough humiliation just by being there, without inviting more. Time, she rather thought, to come out guns blazing. Time to attack.

'I don't know why you felt you had to—say what you d-did...' damn that stutter '...to get me here, I mean. Luckily I was at a loose end tonight—though I do have a dinner date tomorrow,' she inserted hastily. 'But I thought you'd have appreciated, when I didn't come back to the office this afternoon, that I—er—went for an interview for another job!' Oh, Edney, that was brilliant! Just brilliant.

He seemed taken aback. Good! Though she could not help but feel a mite concerned that he appeared to have lost a little bit of his colour. Oh, grief, it was less than a week ago that he'd received that bang on his head!

'You intend to leave?'

That was new—she'd thought he was sacking her! Don't be fooled, Edney, he's as sharp as a tack—you've seen him in action, remember.

'Of course! I—only intended to stay three months!' Now there's a twist! He stared silently at her, as if gauging the truth of what she was saying, but she couldn't take his silent appraisal and felt compelled to carry on. 'Obviously the experience in your office has been invaluable, b-but...' She hesitated, her voice fading, visions coming unsought into her mind—not of putting in a hard day working for him, but the experience of being in his arms. 'S-so, anyway, when I had a phone call last night, inviting me for interview this afternoon—well, I wanted to tell you this morning, only we were so busy and...er—and—er...' Her voice went completely when, watching him, she saw him shake his head from side to side.

'You really are the most outrageous liar!' he remarked. I'm not, she wanted to huff and puff, but wondered if she'd already said too much, so decided to keep quiet. 'Outrageous, and proud,' he added softly. She shrugged her shoulders—what else could she do? 'I've either upset you in some way I haven't fathomed yet, or...' It was Saville who hesitated this time, before attempting to hold her eyes with his, then went on, 'Or I was near to being right, and my eyes didn't deceive me as I was closing the meeting at lunchtime, and...'

'I came here to give you my notice.' She was in there fast, before he could finish and make her humiliation absolute, leaving her pride in shreds by referring to the love he had seen for him in her eyes. 'I wish to resign. I won't be in the office on—'

'You came here, Edney, in response to my last phone call,' Saville cut through her babble of panic. And, taking a long draw of breath—every bit as if he was the one who was nervous, not her—added slowly, 'A phone call which had nothing to do with work.'

Oh, help. He was as good as asking—since she must know it had nothing to do with work—why, since he'd rumbled she'd been telling lies on a grand scale, was she there?

'So, I'm a proud, outrageous liar—with curiosity!' was the best she could manage. But, anxiety biting, she started to think she had said too much, that her tongue, unwary in the heat of the moment sometimes, might run away with her. 'I've said all I'm going to say,' she stated bluntly. 'And—' her glance went to the door '—and you can't keep me here against my will.'

'Normally, I wouldn't attempt to try,' Saville answered, his good-looking face unsmiling as he watched every nuance of expression that crossed her. 'But this, for me, is very far from what I know as normal, so if you'll bear with me?'

Edney had accepted that she was the most confused she had ever been in her life, but just then Saville, this man she loved so wholeheartedly, seemed to be talking in riddles. 'Well, I'm sorry about that, I'm sure!' she offered stiffly, the waspish note she had wanted just not there. She clamped her lips together—she wasn't going to say another word!

'You should be sorry,' Saville responded, but there was none of the harshness she would have expected in his tone. 'Were it not for you, I'd be able to sleep nights!'

Edney's eyes shot wide. 'Add generous to the list— I'm giving you *insomnia?*' Great heavens—she was interrupting his sleep?

She thought she saw his lips twitch, but, with her heart starting to thunder, she wasn't sure of anything any more. His smile didn't make it, however, but Edney felt sorely in need of a chair to sit on when, amazingly, Saville quietly revealed, 'I've admired you from the very first, Edney.'

Her next breath seemed stuck in her chest somewhere. 'You—have?' she gasped.

'You sound as if it's news to you!' he commented. She answered not a word, and he, as decisive as ever, took a step forward and touched her arm. 'I feel on very shaky ground, here. Do take a seat, so I may sit as well.'

Wordlessly, she stared at him. Saville felt he was on shaky ground? There was a positive earthquake going on beneath her feet! Yet, whether he was saying that just as a ploy to have her seated, Edney didn't know. What she did know was that, with the touch of his hand on her arm adding to the general havoc going on inside her, to sit down now seemed quite a good option.

She moved from him, broke his hold, and went to the nearest seat, which happened to be a sofa. And was entirely unprepared when—there were plenty of other chairs and sofas where he could take his ease—Saville opted to come and share her seat. Luckily, she had chosen the four-seater.

Silence reigned for a few moments, reigned and stretched—as though Saville was choosing his words very carefully. But the tension was getting to her, and she just couldn't take it. She had to break it, say something, anything.

'Um—this is a very pleasant room,' she remarked, feeling safe with that kind of comment, indeed certain she couldn't go very far wrong with it.

'It's all the more pleasant for having you here in it,' Saville, whose compliments were as rare as hen's teeth, replied astonishingly. It made her more edgy than ever.

'Cut it out, Craythorne!' she snapped. 'I'm still not coming back to work for you!'

'And I've told you, this has nothing to do with work. It's personal.' Oh, heavens! He was turned, looking intently at her, and she, without fully realising how and why, found she was half turned to him, too. 'It's to do with you and me, and the fact that I shall not rest tonight until I've found out if my—admiration—of you is one-sided.'

She looked away. He waited. She looked back, briefly,

a snatch of a glance. And still he waited. 'Well—when we first met—and since we're talking personally, I—um—naturally I liked the look of you, your—er—manner, or I wouldn't have agreed to go out with you,' she felt pushed to reply, adding quickly, 'Only I didn't get to go out with you—because you turned out to be a—a monster.'

'I deserve that,' Saville accepted without rancour. 'In my defence, though, I saw you the moment I entered Jeremy Knowles's party, knew I wanted to know you, and having thought about you a great deal in the days that followed, I...'

'Did you?' It just sort of slipped from her lips. She gave a little cough, as if those two words were incidental, and, while her heartbeat started to quicken again, she reminded him, 'You rang me from Milan.'

He had not forgotten. 'I worked hard to get back to England sooner rather than later,' Saville confessed, his eyes holding hers.

Sooner rather than later—did he mean so he should see her? Oh, she couldn't believe it! 'You—didn't seem very pleased to see me when you returned and found me working in your office,' she retorted.

To her surprise, he accepted that, as well. 'I was shattered to see you there!' he answered without hesitation. 'The woman I had a dinner date with that night didn't have a job. Yet there you were!'

'You thought I knew, before you returned that Friday, who you were?'

'I didn't know what the devil to think!' he admitted. 'All I knew was that, though I'd been very much anticipating seeing you again that evening, it was not going to happen.'

He'd been looking forward to seeing her! Edney was having a difficult time in keeping her feet on the ground.

'You phoned,' she said. 'You rang and said you couldn't make it.'

'And, while I hardly expected you to be devastated, I have to admit it set me back a bit to hear you seem more pleased than annoyed. "Good" you said, as if it was the best news you'd heard in a long time.'

She'd been furious, she recalled, but wasn't about to tell him that. 'I suspect you could have made it—had you wanted to,' she rejoined quietly.

'Of course,' he answered honestly, giving her the heart-thumping impression that he wanted only to be honest and open with her from now on. 'But how could I? I've never dated anyone from within the organisation. Mainly because I'd never wanted to, but also because of the countless difficulties I envisaged I could be creating. Leaving aside promotion, non-promotion, office politics and the difficulty of getting back to an everyday working footing when the relationship ended, in all fairness, it was not on.'

'So your—um—unwritten rule of no—er—fraternisation outside business had to be applied when you discovered me working in your office?'

'Even though you were the exception that I very much wanted to break that rule for,' he answered, his words causing her heart to pound again, notwithstanding the gentle smile for her that came with them. 'I'd assumed you didn't need to work, but you obviously did, and must have gone through some very thorough training and hard work to get to be Annette's assistant.'

'Er—yes,' she agreed, but just then had matters other than that on her mind.

So, too, it seemed, had Saville, because almost immediately he went on, 'So there was I, dear Edney...' Dear Edney! Oh, help her; she'd be having heart failure at any moment. 'Having decided to stick to my no dating rule, suddenly realising that I was taking unnecessary trips into your office, just to see you, your beautiful face.'

'Oh!' she exclaimed, swallowing hard. 'I—er—didn't—um—know that. More often than not, you just ignored me!'

'You weren't supposed to know it—I barely knew it myself. I certainly wasn't admitting it. All I knew, as I gave you a lift home that Tuesday when we'd been working late and you had car trouble, was that my thinking was going all haywire.'

'It—was?'

Saville moved a little closer—as if she wasn't having enough trouble in the region of her heart! 'You said, as I dropped you off at your home, that, thanks to me, you'd just be able to make your date that night—and I couldn't believe I was actually thinking that if I'd known I'd have left you to find your own way home!'

Edney stared at him in amazement. Then burst out laughing. 'Honestly!' she gasped.

'I couldn't believe my thinking either.'

'I—er—didn't have a date,' she felt honour-bound to admit.

He stared at her. Then, his wonderful mouth turning up at the corners, he said, 'Neither did I.' And, as they sat there smiling at each other, Saville moved the remaining distance, closing the gap between them. Taking her hands in his, he said gruffly, 'I do love you, you know.'

'Oh, Saville,' she whispered tremulously.

'Do you care for me?' he questioned tautly.

He must know that she did! But, 'I'm—I'm scared,' she admitted. She just couldn't believe that he loved her—it was just too incredible.

'What of?' he demanded. 'Tell me, little love, and I'll sort out whatever frightens you.'

'How can you love me?'

'How can I not?' Saville answered.

'How do you know?' She was still scared. She loved him quite desperately. But it just couldn't be the same for him—could it?

'I do. I just do. It's there in my heart—and won't go away,' Saville answered tenderly. He carried on, when it seemed she needed more convincing before she could believe, accept, wholeheartedly what he was saying, 'It's just there, Edney. There in everything. There in my head, there in the jealousy that assaults me, the...'

'You've been jealous?' Stunned, she stared at him.

'I've seldom been clear of it,' Saville owned. And, while Edney continued to stare at him, he went on, 'Even while I was not prepared to accept that most unpalatable of emotions for what it was, there was I, not liking at all to hear of your weekend trips away.'

'To visit my mother!' she exclaimed.

'I didn't know that then.' He smiled, and while her heart flipped in one of its crazy little somersaults at his smile, he confessed, 'nor that the man you embraced in the car park was your stepbrother.'

'You were jealous of Miles?'

'Jealous, and heartsore,' he replied. 'Jealous—only two days before you'd been in my arms then, two days later, you had your arms all round somebody else! So, all right. I still hadn't admitted to myself what my feelings for you were—but that didn't stop the gut-wrenching from going on.'

'Oh, Saville,' she whispered, and was only capable of sitting there staring, her insides going wild, when he raised one of her hands to his lips and tenderly kissed it.

'And heartsore, sweet love,' he murmured throatily, 'to know that I'd almost made you cry because, as jealous as fury, I bruised your sensitivity when I challenged you about him.'

'You weren't to know that less than an hour before that I'd discovered that I—um…' Her voice failed her.

'There's a shyness in your eyes, a pink glow to your face,' Saville took up, everything about him alert to her. 'What happened an hour before, Edney?' he asked, an urgent tone there in his voice, this man who was shrewd, aware—and sensitive.

Did she dare believe him—dared she not? She wanted to believe him, wanted to believe in his sensitivity to her—sensitivity because he loved her. She took a very nervous breath and knew whatever happened from now on, she was going to have to be very brave and, as incredible as it seemed, trust him, trust that he meant it when he said that he loved her. 'I—um—you'd gone to lunch—we'd had a bit of a—terse—sort of conversation, centred on the fact I wasn't going to work that weekend, and as you went off to lunch, well, I just—sort of—knew that I…' The words got stuck.

'That you?' Saville urged, as if sensing that something pretty momentous was coming.

'That I—um—quite—liked you.'

'Wretched woman—*liked?*'

'Well, quite loved you, really,' she said on a gulp of breath—and was hauled into his arms for her trouble.

'Oh, sweet, sweet, Edney,' he breathed in her ear. 'I've been half out of my mind since first I thought I saw—didn't see—was I totally crazy to believe I saw what I wanted to see in your face?'

'Lunchtime?'

'Lunchtime,' he agreed, pulling back to gently kiss her and, while her heart was drumming madly, drawing back to look at her, a world of love for her there in his eyes. 'It's incredible,' he breathed, his eyes adoring. 'I'm still having the greatest trouble taking in that, after the way I've been to you, you actually love me.'

'I—can't seem to help it,' Edney confessed with a shaky smile.

'You're wonderful,' he murmured, and tenderly kissed her. For long moments, then, they just held and looked at each other. Then Saville was confessing, 'I thought— at the end of this morning's meeting, when, in the middle of my closing remarks, I looked at you and saw in your eyes what I later had to grimly hang on and hope I saw— that my heart would stop.'

'I was horrified that you'd seen.' She smiled, and Saville just had to gently kiss her again.

'And I, though my heart beat suffocatingly, was desperately trying to remember what it was I was supposed to be saying, while at the same time holding a picture of you in my mind and heart of that look in your eyes. I had to look away in order to try and get some control, and the next time I looked you'd gone.'

'I took advantage of Winthrop Butler, Felix and one or two others who went over to talk to you to get out of there,' she owned.

'You almost gave me heart failure,' he complained lovingly. 'I'm afraid I was rather short with everyone as I chased after you.'

'I saw you!' she gasped. 'I thought you were rushing to get to the restaurant I'd…'

'Restaurant! Who could eat? I came after you—but you'd gone. You saw me?' he questioned.

. 'I raced to my office, dropped my notes and grabbed my bag, and felt too terrified that I might see you if I waited for the lift, so I belted for the stairs—and caught a glimpse of you looking nowhere but where you were going, when I was at the bottom of the first flight.'

'You do realise I've wasted a whole afternoon trying to find you,' he said severely.

'I stopped you working!'

'To the blazes with work. I meant an afternoon ringing

your home number without success. An afternoon of pacing the carpet trying to hang on to that picture of that look in your eyes.'

She smiled, no longer terrified. More, she was enchanted. 'You thought I'd bolt for home?'

'At first I was so incredulous I just wasn't thinking at all. Then I decided, logically, that all you'd done was go to lunch. Only I wasn't feeling very logical, so I broke off pacing to go and again indulge in what had, of late, become something of a habit with me.'

'What?' she asked, foxed.

'Looking out of my window to check if you were either driving in or driving out of the car park,' he explained, and when she looked at him in startled delight, he growled, 'So, okay, I'm smitten.' He seemed to love her gurgle of laughter, for he kissed her again, then resumed. 'I knew—on Monday I admitted—that I was in love with you.'

'You knew then?' she questioned softly.

'After you'd left that afternoon,' he owned with a loving look. 'But I couldn't believe it—it's never happened to me before,' he confessed, to her further delight. He stretched out a hand and almost reverently touched her face. 'So, on Tuesday, I flew to Milan—and found that my love for you was a constant travelling companion.'

'Oh, how lovely that sounds!' she exclaimed softly.

'Oh, my darling, you've no idea of the devil of a time I've had resisting the urge to call you. I picked up the phone many times to do just that, but was so nervous every time, of tripping myself up, that each time I put the phone down again.'

'Oh, Saville,' she uttered sensitively, 'I've been afraid of giving myself away—but you?'

Saville smiled and planted a kiss to a corner of her mouth. 'I knew, of course, that there was some pretty spectacular chemistry between us—you're blushing,' he inserted with obvious delight, 'but I wanted more than that. I needed to know if you felt more for me than chemistry. Which is why I decided that when I got back from Italy I'd ask you to have dinner with me tonight, and...'

'You were going to ask me out tonight!' she exclaimed. And, remembering how cool and impersonal he had been with her that morning, 'I'd never have guessed,' she informed him impudently.

He grinned. 'Have a heart, my darling. You'd got me so I didn't know where I was!'

'I had?'

'I was, and am, quite desperately in love with you—and those, save that there was one very important meeting to be got out of the way this morning, were about the only two facts I was sure about. With my head and heart so all over the place, I tried for logic, and decided to finish the meeting first, then I would be free to concentrate solely on us. Perhaps dinner tonight. Perhaps if I was lucky—if only I could be that lucky—I might get the chance to see you Saturday and Sunday—you weren't due to go to Bristol, so dare I hope?'

'Good heavens!' she gasped, amazed at his thinking.

'There was I this morning, at my window watching for your arrival—which gave me just a few short minutes to get myself under control before you came into my office. I so dearly wanted to take you in my arms—which is why I didn't so much as dare look up when I called you in.'

'Saville!' she gasped—and knew then that she could trust completely everything he had been saying, and, incredible as she still found it, that he was in love with her.

'Which is why, and how, I knew that you'd driven to work in your car,' he went on, 'and why my insides went into a rampaging panic when, looking out of my window

to watch for your return at lunchtime, I saw that your
car was not where you'd parked it.'

'You knew I'd gone home?'

'It was more instinct, I think. I somehow knew, without being properly aware, that you never took your car
out at lunchtimes. So, I waited, did some more pacing
up and down, and waited, and when you didn't come
back at two I began to hope again. Reasoning—if I
wasn't totally deluding myself—that it could mean that
you did love me, that you knew I'd seen your love and
that you, my proud darling, were determined that it was
the last I would see of you.'

'What did you decide?' she asked prettily.

'Decide? Wretched woman, I was at my most unde-
cided. Should I follow you? Should I ring? Perhaps I'd
got it wrong. No, I wasn't having that, couldn't have
that. I'd stick to my original plan—ring you, and ask
you to have dinner with me tonight.'

'Oh, Saville—and I wouldn't speak to you,' she whispered contritely.

'You were most unfriendly,' he teased severely. 'I
guess I've got the fact that your father was in to thank
that you came to the phone at all those first two times.'

'I'm sorry,' she apologised nicely, and, encouraged by
the love in his eyes, she reached up and kissed him. 'I
didn't think you'd ring again,' she confessed.

'What else was I to do? I'd called at your home and
just refused to believe you weren't in...'

'I was skulking upstairs,' she confessed, glorying in
the feeling of being able to tell him anything.

Saville smiled a wonderful smile, but was totally serious when he revealed, 'And I was frustrated beyond
bearing.'

'You rang from your car phone?'

'I had to do something. It was unbearable doing nothing. But I realised that since it seemed you weren't pre-

pared to have any sort of a conversation with me—my previous two calls allowed me just one sentence each before you cut me off—whatever I said had to be short and to the point.'

'You said, "Edney, I love you"—and I couldn't believe it.'

'And I went home to do some more floor-pacing while I tried to think up some other way of getting to see you tonight. My heart went wild when my doorbell rang. Was it you? Wasn't it you? Had it worked? My plan was that because I'd told you I love you, you'd know, if love me you did, that you had nothing to fear. I came to the door, fighting like the very devil to hide my feelings should it not be you. But there you were—and I knew I was not going to let you go—not now.'

'I'm—er—glad I came,' she murmured, and as Saville gathered her close once more she had nothing else to say for quite a while as they kissed and clung to each other, hearts thundering, the joy of just being together washing away all pain and anguish of the past.

And yet, to her amazement, it seemed that when she had just wholeheartedly returned his kisses, Saville still needed reassurance of her feelings for him. 'You are truly in love with me, my darling?' he questioned quietly as they drew back but, still in each other's arms, sat and feasted their eyes on one another.

'Most definitely, definitely,' she answered with a loving smile.

'When did it start?'

She knew the feeling, too, of wanting to know more of this wondrous love they shared, but cared for him more than enough to answer anything he asked. 'Almost from the beginning, I think,' she said. 'I liked your sensitivity—that first night we met, when you so very tenderly kissed me, in a healing way.' She smiled a warm smile. 'Then you rang, asking me out to dinner, when you were in Milan. Usually, I'm just not given to getting over-excited at the thought of a first date, but that time my heart started beating ten to the dozen.'

'Tell me more,' he ordered.

'Well, we didn't get to go out on a first date, and you went decidedly off me...'

'Never!'

'And I found myself wishing that things were different between us.'

'Because you were falling in love with me?'

Edney shook her head. 'I didn't know then what was unsettling me so—making me so restless. Er—though I'll admit to—um—feeling my share of jealousy too.' And, seeing Saville's expression go from sheer surprise to grinning delight, 'Trust you to look pleased!' she laughed. 'There was I, having a meal with an old friend of my stepbrother, and in you come, a stunning brunette in tow, making me all churned up inside—and I started to realise you had some sort of effect on me.'

'I couldn't be more pleased about that,' Saville countered, but—and there was not a smile about him now '—do you usually go in for hand-holding with your stepbrother's friends?'

'You're jealous!' she accused.

'Why wouldn't I be? You as good as told me you'd slept with the hand-holding varmint!'

Edney was taken aback—until she remembered the construction he must have put on her saying that she had gone to bed early that night. 'I didn't. I didn't sleep with him!' she said in a hurry.

'I know that *now*!' Saville assured her with equal speed. 'My sweet darling, don't I know it now? Have you any idea of the cold sweat you put me in when, in that hotel in Copenhagen, I discovered you'd been with no other man.'

'You threw me out!' she reminded him. 'You told me

to go to bed. To be honest,' she confessed, 'I didn't understand then, and I don't understand now. You were, have been, so changeable. I don't—'

'Oh, my sweet innocent,' Saville cut in tenderly. 'Yes,' he owned, 'I suppose from where you're viewing it I have been changeable. If you'll allow me a defence, though, you were starting to get me so much, I didn't know where I was half the time.'

'Don't leave it there,' she begged mischievously.

'Oh, my dear, I can see I'm going to have trouble with you,' he grinned, but, as she'd requested, he went on, 'There was I, finding you working in my office, and knowing in my head that I was going to have to cool it. While all the time my heart was telling me something totally different.'

'I love you,' she said, purely because she couldn't help it.

Saville kissed her, and kissed her again, and looked as if he might kiss her a third time. Then, as if wanting everything said and out of the way quickly, he pulled a little away from her and resumed, 'So, if I'm going to treat you just as I would any other employee—why was I going in to your office constantly to take a look at you? Why was I getting all chewed up inside because my cousin Felix was clearly trying to date you?'

'You've been jealous of your cousin?' she asked in surprise.

'Murderously jealous!' he admitted, explaining, when her eyes shot wide, 'I'd had an invitation to the party, too but couldn't make it—until I heard you agree to go with Felix. I just couldn't believe myself when I rang our hosts to say I could make it after all.'

Edney beamed, but recalled, 'You were furious with me.'

'I was furious, full stop!' Saville corrected. 'And

ready to throw Felix to the other side of the room when I saw him kissing your neck.'

'I objected too,' she thought she might mention. 'Only you accused me of encouraging him.'

'Forgive me,' he apologised. 'By the time I'd crossed the floor to you I'd managed to gain sufficient self-control not to separate Felix from his teeth. Which left me, having got you away from him, laying into you instead. But by no means was I going to allow him to drive you home, nor was I going to have him kissing your neck in the back of my car.'

'Oh, Saville!' she sighed. Then suddenly she blinked. 'You said... Did you know Felix's car was out of action before he did?'

'I think I have to confess that, yes, I did, since it was me who put it out of action.'

'You mean...!' she gasped. 'You disabled Felix's car—deliberately!'

'As I said—I wasn't having him driving you home—it was a simple enough matter to put it right when I got back.'

She was stunned! 'Saville Craythorne, for shame!' she exclaimed. 'So that's why you had me sitting up front—pretending you couldn't remember where I lived. Oh!' Something else suddenly occurred to her. 'I thought, when you asked for my key and seemed in a rush to get rid of me, it was because you wanted to get back to your blonde companion—but it wasn't that, was it?'

'My "blonde companion" is a good friend and nothing more—safe, because I happen to know that her heart belongs to another,' he explained, with a sympathetic look, and Edney guessed he had witnessed the tinge of green in her eyes. She smiled at him for his understanding, and he went on, 'But, while I still wasn't admitting the eruption of feeling that was going on inside me for you, there was no way I was going to allow my cousin to part from you with a kiss.'

'That makes two of us,' she laughed, feeling stunned that all this had gone on without her suspecting a thing about it.

'Oh, my dear one, I do love you so,' Saville breathed—and they just had to kiss. 'Do you know what you do to me, woman?' Saville growled as they broke apart. 'I haven't the smallest notion of what I was telling you.'

'You—um—I think you were saying, er, explaining about your changeable disposition,' she whispered dreamily.

'So I was,' he smiled. 'Though not that it's any kind of an explanation. I was as changeable with myself as with you. Forever fighting my attraction to you. I clearly remember, weeks back—it was a Friday, that Friday Annette went early. That Friday when I convinced myself it was nothing to do with me if I didn't see you again until Monday—so why was I arming myself with an excuse, should I have needed one, and giving in to the compulsion to have one last word with you?'

'Oh,' Edney sighed blissfully, and then recalled the night in question, that Friday that Annette had left early. 'We parted enemies!' she exclaimed—it had been the Friday after her date with Graeme, when she had told Saville she had gone to bed early. 'Graeme, by the way,' she felt in all fairness she should declare, 'is Miles's friend. He's, well, he's still suffering from a divorce he didn't want,' she also mentioned, 'so we are—er—just friends.'

'I'm very pleased to hear it!' Saville stated, something in the way he said it causing her to realise that Saville would at some time have asked her more about Graeme. But she only loved Saville more when, as if wanting nothing hiding in dark corners between them, he revealed, 'The brunette. I only dated her the one time.' And, with a teasing look, he added, 'An impudent redhead who a week later had the spirit to go for my jugular somehow dulled my interest in anybody else. I really think, my dear one, that Friday, when with your gorgeous eyes flashing sparks you went for me, was the day when I started to fall in love with you.'

Her mouth fell open—she had thought him about to dismiss her that Friday! 'Truly?'

'Given, of course, that I was extraordinarily attracted to you from that moment of first seeing you, I'm sure of it,' he replied. 'It seems to me now that it was after that Friday that I began my routine of checking the car park, of leaving my office door open—accidentally on purpose—so I might catch the occasional glimpse of you.'

Edney expelled a sigh of pure rapture. 'Am I dreaming?' she asked.

'I feel much the same way,' Saville breathed, and tenderly they kissed.

'You were saying?' Edney found out of a mildly ecstatic somewhere.

'I—was saying, I believe,' Saville took up, sounding as if he wasn't very sure now where he had left off, 'that you, my darling, were starting to get to me in a big way. I well remember, when Annette was on holiday, how the day before my trip to Germany you and I had been working late. There was, I accept now, no reason at all why we should have dinner together. But I was determined it was work, not pleasure, that we could work while we ate...'

'You—were fooling yourself?' she suggested, a mite shyly.

'And how!' he smiled, and confessed, 'I watched you drive away that night and knew myself to be quite enchanted by you.'

Her beautiful eyes went wide with wonder. His confession, however, called for a confession from her. 'And I drove home realising that, away from the office, you were unbelievably charming.' Saville tenderly traced gentle fingers down one side of her face, and Edney basked in the warmth of his love. 'You were back to being an unfriendly brute when you returned,' she reminded him teasingly.

'Try not to be too hard on me, little love,' Saville asked of her. 'I was, to put it mildly, forever having to put thoughts of you away from me while I was in Germany. I'd enjoyed your company so much at dinner, yet told myself it mustn't happen again. I'd realised by the time I was flying home again that I had to keep things strictly business between us.' Edney was so enraptured she could only vaguely remember she had thought on similar lines herself a few months ago. 'In the interests of your career, let alone anything else,' he went on, 'I had to put some distance between us.'

'You certainly did that.'

'You think it was easy?'

'Tell me,' she urged, growing more confident in his love by the minute, but just adoring to know more.

'You've no idea how I had to strive to hide my pleasure at seeing you again. Strictly business, I kept saying to myself. Then, a couple of days later, you scalded your hand, and in my concern it seemed instinctive to hold you in my arms while you battled with the pain. Believe me, my darling, there was nothing sexual in my need to comfort you, to hold you in your time of pain. But eventually alarm sirens were starting to sound—strictly business! There was no way I would have held Annette so, had she been the casualty.'

'You were—er—a bit terse afterwards,' she remarked—with masterly understatement.

He grinned. 'Why wouldn't I be? I still hadn't got

myself fully together when Felix called, and while I was
sure I didn't give a damn that he was taking you to a
party, I found, when I'd had no intention of going to
that party, that I couldn't keep away.'

'You were hating me?'

'How could I hate you? You're everything to me,' he
breathed, and Edney went all weak inside.

'You weren't saying that when you saw me at the
airport and not Annette,' she somehow managed to remind him softly.

'Why would I? All I knew then was that I was going
to need all my powers of concentration for the job in
hand, and there you were—to distract me.'

'You say the loveliest things,' she laughed.

'Witch!' he becalled her. 'So there was I, trying hard
to deny how my heart seemed to rejoice when I saw you
at the airport—and I guessed from your luggage that you
would be assisting me on the Copenhagen trip—so at
the same time, I had to do my best to remain aloof.'

'We kissed,' she murmured of that lovely memory.

'Indeed we did,' he said softly. 'That was the shortest,
yet longest, two days of my life. Business, I kept telling
myself, strictly business—but it was a poor show. I was
enjoying your company.'

'Were you?'

'Believe it. Even if I was having trouble sleeping,
even while I wasn't admitting it, I wanted to see you. I
was wide awake; sleep was a million miles away...' He
broke off. 'Are you going to forgive me for calling the
desk and asking them to give you a wake-up call.'

'You put the alarm call in because you wanted to see
me?'

'Well,' he defended, 'you did have a lot to get through
that day.'

'May I tell you again that I love you?'

'Oh, dear love, keep saying it,' he encouraged. They

kissed then, and kissed some more—until at last Saville
pulled back. 'I'm attempting with all I've got to do this
right—it's my first experience of loving, as I mentioned,'
he said throatily, 'but if we kiss much more, sweetheart,
I'm going to lose it.'

'I'll try to behave,' she murmured, with as much prim-
ness as she could muster.

'For such an innocent, you can lead a man very much
astray,' Saville chided lovingly.

'You're thinking of that Saturday night in
Copenhagen?'

'That Saturday when I knew I should let you return
to your room—but it seemed beyond me to let you go.
I wanted more of your company—so the panic you put
me in...'

'Panic?'

'Lovely Edney, I'd been doing my poor best to stay
aloof from you—an impossible task, I should have
known at the outset. But so much for my staying aloof;
there we were, about to go into my bedroom, when you
suddenly scared me half to death by revealing just how
innocent you are!'

'That scared you?'

'Little darling, I desired you like crazy. Yet there I
was, your employer, with you in a foreign country, you
under my protection, and what was I doing? Seducing
you! If ever I needed anything to bring me to my senses,
poor though they were at the time, the fact of trying to
take in that if we carried on the way we were I would
be guilty of robbing you of your innocence did the trick.'
From what she could remember of it, and her memory
of that time was astonishingly clear, the seduction had
been mutual. 'I barely slept that night, either,' he smiled.

'Because of me?'

'Yes, because of you,' he answered. 'I needed a clear
head, but thoughts of you, the way you were, are, were

clouding my vision. Yet I had to think of you. Only a short while earlier you'd asked me how your three-month trial was going—when, in my head, I already regarded you as a permanent member of staff. I—'

'You did?' she butted in delightedly.

'My dear, after the excellent way you coped in Annette's absence, there was no doubt about it. But your question that night only served to endorse for me that you were career-minded, and that I *must* keep matters between us strictly on a business footing—only I had reckoned without you.'

'What did *I* do?' she questioned, startled.

'You, my proud darling, were so distant the next morning—every bit as though our lovemaking had never happened—and there was I, in danger of losing sight of the way it was going to be in future before I started. I was well and truly peeved, sweet love, that after being so responsive to me the night before you were now treating me as though, outside the office, I didn't exist.'

'If it's any consolation, I drove home that day close to tears about *your* attitude, and hating you because you could do that to me,' she admitted, and knew herself well beloved when, with a groan, Saville pulled her close up against him.

'Oh, my dear love, I'll never hurt you like that again,' he promised, and kissed her.

It was again bliss, utter bliss, to be cradled in his arms. Edney never wanted to move. But his talk of hurt reminded her, and she twisted to look at him. 'How's your poor head?' she asked seriously.

'You're referring to the cricket ball incident? As good as new,' he assured her. 'Though I'll admit I wasn't feeling too clever when it first happened. But the minute I started to recover I wanted out of that hospital.'

'I'm glad it was me you rang to come and get you,' she smiled.

'Dear Edney, when there were several other people aside from my parents I could have phoned—they simply didn't enter the equation. You were the only one I wanted to see.'

'Oh, that's lovely,' she sighed. 'Though you must have been feeling very groggy.'

'Just enough to make me realise that if I was going to be up to the Milan trip on Tuesday, and today's detailed meeting, that I'd better take the consultant's advice and rest my head on Monday. I was so glad you stayed,' he murmured softly.

'You told me to go home, but I couldn't.'

'And, even though I was more myself come morning, I found I didn't want you to leave. I didn't know then why I should feel this great need to have you stay with me—I just couldn't bear to let you go.'

'You were still feeling a bit groggy?' Edney suggested softly.

'Maybe,' he accepted. 'But if you went, and didn't come back, I wouldn't see you again before Friday. I, my dear, was very close to admitting my true feelings for you.'

'Were you always this stubborn?' she asked huskily, starting to feel no end guilty—now that she knew of his love—at her heartlessness in leaving him that morning. 'I did ring you from the office,' she reminded him.

'And I was missing you.'

'I came back, as I promised I would,' she smiled. 'I brought some post, and the paperwork you wanted.'

'Oh, you did, my love—and all I knew then was that I was never so happy than when I was with you.' Her breath caught—what a wonderful thing for him to say. 'Is it any wonder, dearest Edney, that I lost total sight of all my vows to stick to business?'

'You mean when I kissed you?'

'When you kissed me, keeping things strictly business flew out of the window.'

'I forgot too—or almost did—about your injury, I mean. Your head. I wasn't sure the stimulation of—er—um—lovemaking was good for you,' she mentioned, unsure what to make of the stunned surprise on his face. 'I started to feel sure that it couldn't be right for you—you were still supposed to be recovering, and—'

'*Now* you tell me!' Saville broke in, a grin on his face stretching from ear to ear.

'What did I tell you?' She had thought she had done with confusion, but she was starting to feel it again.

'I thought you put a stop to our lovemaking because you didn't think it was right for you! Because you were *unsure*!' he revealed—and it was her turn to experience stunned surprise.

'Oh!' she gasped, but found a grin too, as she declared, 'You made a wanton of me and for a second time threw me out, Mr Craythorne.'

'What a delight you are to me!' he breathed. 'And you—a wanton? My dear, you have no idea of the spellbinding innocence of your response.' He just had to break off to gently kiss her again. But he pulled back to look deeply into her lovely eyes. 'As for throwing you out a second time, my heart's darling, even though I knew that there was no way I was going to coerce you or persuade you against your will, I have to confess I wanted you so badly I could barely live with it. I was losing it fast—the only way to cope was to have you gone, with all speed.'

'Oh!' she exclaimed. 'You—you were all right—after I'd gone—on Monday?'

He shook his head. Alarmed, she stared at him. But Saville quickly eased her fears. 'How could I be all right? No sooner did I get myself on an even keel again when, suddenly—and it was no longer a case of just admitting—it was there, with sledgehammer force: the realisation that I was quite desperately in love with you.'

Edney sighed. 'I'm so glad,' she murmured.

'Which pleases me,' Saville returned, but went on to remind her of something which he had not forgotten she'd said when she first arrived. 'But what about this dinner date you have tomorrow. Can you break it?'

'Er…' She hesitated, doubtful.

'Edney, I believe you love me, but it isn't doing anything for that green-eyed monster sitting on my shoulder to know that tomorrow night some man might be taking…'

'Oh, it's not another man,' she rushed in quickly. 'Mrs Andrews—you remember Mrs Andrews—my father's friend? Well, she's invited me to dinner with her and my father tomorrow evening, and…'

'That's a relief,' Saville butted in with a smile. But suddenly his expression was deadly serious when, with his eyes fixed on her face, he asked, 'How about I book a table for the four of us to celebrate somewhere?'

'Celebrate?' she queried, not surprised, the way her heart was dancing, that she was growing confused again.

Which was why she was totally staggered when, with no change in the seriousness of his expression, Saville replied, 'We could celebrate our engagement, couldn't we, Edney?'

'Engagement?' she gasped.

'Our brief engagement, prior to our marriage,' he stated firmly, a kind of tension starting to mix with his seriousness as he waited.

'Er…' Her heart was pounding so badly she could barely think.

'Say yes, Edney. Say you'll marry me,' he urged. 'I love you. I can't bear not to have you with me,' he pressed. 'My life is soulless when you're not here. Please say yes, my love.'

'Oh, I love you so,' she whispered tremulously.

'Is that yes?' he asked tensely, and it seemed quite incredible to her that he couldn't see that, oh, yes, yes, yes, the answer was yes!

'I'd like very much to marry you,' she answered mistily, and was immediately held close to his heart for long, long seconds.

Then Saville kissed her. 'Thank you, my lovely darling,' he breathed, and kissed her tenderly again before drawing back to look deeply into her eyes. 'If your father's gone to bed when we get to your home, I'll come and see him in the morning,' he asserted—as she well knew, he was a man who got things done.

Although she suddenly realised, with yet more quickening of her heartbeat, that since Saville was talking of them having but a 'brief engagement' prior to their marriage, by the sound of it there would be small time for delay. 'That—um—sounds rather good,' she smiled.

And Saville just had to pause to kiss her again. 'And then, if it's all right with you,' he suggested, 'perhaps we could have a celebratory lunch in Bristol with your mother.'

'Oh, Saville!' Edney sighed. 'I always knew you were sensitive. You've realised my mother truly wouldn't like it if my father's friend met you before she did.'

He smiled, and with a light kiss to the tip of her dainty nose, drew her to her feet. 'Come on, my love, we've a lot to do.'

'Er—we have?'

'I hope you're not arguing, Miss Rayner—soon to be Mrs Craythorne,' he said with mock severity. 'Your family tomorrow; my family on Sunday.' And, while her heart was already bursting with joy, 'Then on Monday we'll have time to think about us, and that early wedding date.'

Her heart wasn't merely bursting with joy, it was overflowing with joy. 'I don't think I'd argue with that,' she answered dreamily—and was lovingly kissed.

Take 2 bestselling love stories FREE

Plus get a FREE surprise gift!

Special Limited-Time Offer

Mail to Harlequin Reader Service®

3010 Walden Avenue
P.O. Box 1867
Buffalo, N.Y. 14240-1867

YES! Please send me 2 free Harlequin Romance® novels and my free surprise gift. Then send me 6 brand-new novels every month, which I will receive months before they appear in bookstores. Bill me at the low price of $2.90 each plus 25¢ delivery and applicable sales tax if any*. That's the complete price, and a saving of over 10% off the cover prices—quite a bargain! I understand that accepting the books and gift places me under no obligation ever to buy any books. I can always return a shipment and cancel at any time. Even if I never buy another book from Harlequin, the 2 free books and the surprise gift are mine to keep forever.

116 HEN CH66

Name	(PLEASE PRINT)	
Address		Apt. No.
City	State	Zip

This offer is limited to one order per household and not valid to present Harlequin Romance® subscribers. *Terms and prices are subject to change without notice. Sales tax applicable in N.Y.

UROM-98 ©1990 Harlequin Enterprises Limited

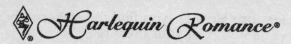
Harlequin Romance®

We're proud to announce the "birth" of a brand-
new series full of babies, bachelors and happy-
ever-afters: *Daddy Boom.* Meet gorgeous heroes
who are about to discover that there's a first time
for everything—even fatherhood!

Starting in February 1999 we'll be bringing you one
Daddy Boom title every other month.

February 1999: **BRANNIGAN'S BABY**
by Grace Green

April 1999: **DADDY AND DAUGHTERS**
by Barbara McMahon

We'll also be bringing you deliciously cute
Daddy Boom books by Lucy Gordon,
Kate Denton, Leigh Michaels and a special
Christmas story from Emma Richmond.

Who says bachelors and babies don't mix?

Available wherever Harlequin books are sold.

HARLEQUIN®
Makes any time special ™

Question: How do you find the sexy cowboy of your dreams?

Answer: Read on....

Texas Grooms Wanted!
is a brand-new miniseries from

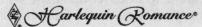
Harlequin Romance®

Meet three very special heroines who are all looking for very special Texas men—their future husbands! Good men may be hard to find, but these women have experts on hand. They've all signed up with the Yellow Rose Matchmakers. The oldest and the best matchmaking service in San Antonio, Texas, the Yellow Rose guarantees to find any woman her perfect partner....

So for the cutest cowboys in the whole state of Texas, look out for:

HAND-PICKED HUSBAND
by Heather MacAllister in January 1999

BACHELOR AVAILABLE!
by Ruth Jean Dale in February 1999

THE NINE-DOLLAR DADDY
by Day Leclaire in March 1999

Only cowboys need apply...

Available wherever
Harlequin Romance books
are sold.

Sexy, desirable and...a daddy?

THE AUSTRALIANS

Stories of romance Australian-style, guaranteed to fulfill that sense of adventure!

This February 1999 look for

Baby Down Under

by **Ann Charlton**

Riley Templeton was a hotshot Queensland lawyer with a reputation for ruthlessness and a weakness for curvaceous blondes. Alexandra Page was everything that Riley *wasn't* looking for in a woman, but when she finds a baby on her doorstep that leads her to the dashing lawyer, he begins to see the virtues of brunettes—and babies!

The Wonder from Down Under: where spirited women win the hearts of Australia's most independent men!

Available February 1999
at your favorite retail outlet.

HARLEQUIN®
Makes any time special ™

MEN at WORK

All work and no play?
Not these men!

January 1999
SOMETHING WORTH KEEPING by Kathleen Eagle
He worked with iron and steel, and was as wild as the mustangs that were his passion. She was a high-class horse trainer from the East. Was her gentle touch enough to tame his unruly heart?

February 1999
HANDSOME DEVIL by Joan Hohl
His roguish good looks and intelligence drew women like magnets, but Luke Branson was having too much fun to marry again. Then Selena McInnes strolled before him and turned his life upside down!

March 1999
STARK LIGHTNING by Elaine Barbieri
The boss's daughter was ornery, stubborn and off-limits for cowboy Branch Walker! But Valentine was also nearly impossible to resist. Could they negotiate a truce...or a surrender?

Available at your favorite retail outlet!

MEN AT WORK™

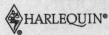 

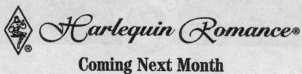

Coming Next Month

#3539 BACHELOR AVAILABLE! Ruth Jean Dale
Cody James was tall, sexy and handsome—he took Emily Kirkwood's breath away. Too bad that Emily hadn't joined the Yellow Rose Matchmakers to find a man but to write a Valentine's story on... well...how to get a man. Only, Cody *was* available...and perhaps what this story needed was a little in-depth research!

Texas Grooms Wanted! *Only cowboys need apply!*

#3540 BOARDROOM PROPOSAL Margaret Way
It's the job of her dreams, but can Eve Copeland believe that she won it fairly and squarely? Her new boss, after all, has a secret he'd go to great lengths to conceal....

#3541 HER HUSBAND-TO-BE Leigh Michaels
Deke Oliver was convinced Danielle was trying to manipulate him into marriage—just because they'd jointly inherited a property...and were forced to live together under the same roof! But Deke wasn't husband material, and Danielle simply *had* to convince him that she wasn't dreaming of wedding bells!

#3542 BRANNIGAN'S BABY Grace Green
When Luke Brannigan asked Whitney for help, she was torn. On the one hand, she wanted to get as far away as possible from this annoyingly gorgeous man, who insisted on flirting with her. On the other, how could she refuse to help when Luke was obviously struggling to bring up his adorable baby son?

Daddy Boom—*Who says bachelors and babies don't mix?*